TO WHOM IT MAY CONCERN:

love.. luck.. my bad!

TO WHOM IT MAY CONCERN:

love.. luck.. my bad!

Shariq Iqbal

Srishti
PUBLISHERS & DISTRIBUTORS

Srishti Publishers & Distributors
N-16, C. R. Park
New Delhi 110 019
srishtipublishers@gmail.com

First published by Srishti Publishers & Distributors in 2009
10th impression, 2011

Typeset in AGaramond 11pt. by Suresh Kumar Sharma at Srishti

Printed and bound in India

Acknowledgements

If it's as simple as a 'thank you', then first of all I thank my parents, for bearing with such a strange son like me. Infact not for merely bearing, but for always finding some reasons to unconditionally love me, despite my inherent flaws.

Likewise I'd thank Saima, for being the most merciless critic, yet being the most rocking sister ever. Sis, thanks for withstanding those grueling discussions over late night coffees... You made this happen!

Lots of love to Faiza, simply for making life a journey worthwhile.

Though it's terrible to bring about formalities in friendships, I'll still thank the entire band of my kick-ass friends, for the good ol' backbench days, for the innumerous meaningless laughters, and for all those proxies that are very much a reason behind this book.

One and all at Bangalore Mirror, for giving me the first thrill to see my name in print, and also for stitching the holes in my pocket!

Srishti Publishers' entire team, for believing in my work and giving me the break.

God, for being there when I least expected. Mr. Viqar Ahmad, for being a God-sent.

Strangely enough, I'd thank the Bangalore city, for throwing me into the most rocky journey of my life, and for never bothering me throughout.

And lastly but immensely, I thank *you*, for holding this book, for being the reason behind it, for a bond that starts after this page... and goes on beyond it.

"Every pleasures got an edge of pain, so pay for your ticket and don't complain."

– Bob Dylan

Don't drink and drive… Smoke weed and fly!

"Gawwwd…what time is it?" I asked myself getting up from deep sleep. I had probably never found my throat so dry, as I began to pour water into itself and doubted whether my thirst would ever be quenched. I had almost forgotten where I was when a shrill voice bought me to life, "Hey! You done with your sleep? All your friends are gone and you are still sleeping! When are you gonna get up?"

With partially open and sticky eyes, I tried to recognize the person at the door. "Hey Neelam, What time is it? It's still early dawn *yar*." I said with a creaking voice, noticing the dark outside but surprised at the sound of bustling traffic.

"Dawn? What dawn? Hah… You think this is morning darkness? It's almost 10 pm into the night! You have been sleeping here since yesterday evening… Both your friends went a long time ago in the afternoon! What are you saying? Are you serious?" she said walking towards me and patted twice on my stubbled cheek.

Suddenly I realized she was right, staring at the wooden walls of the cramped and smelly room, I wondered how I had slept for so long on this damp and malodorous bed and hadn't feel a thing.

Hysterically getting up from the bed, I put on my t-shirt and shoes in a hurry, slipped on my wallet and cell into my pocket, and rushed out of the door down the narrow staircase, finally out on to the road.

Briskly walking, settling my hair and still wondering how I had slept so long, the chilled Bangalore winter breeze shivered my chest and made me run back to get the jacket I left in the room.

Grabbing the jacket lying ruffled on the bed and neglecting the socks I forgot to wear, I finally ran out of that humid attic, atlast running towards *Paras Cinema*, a place which had been re-running old Rajnikanth films for years now, and pulled in almost house-full crowds everytime, something which the best of recent flicks failed to do.

Well not here to watch the movie, infact never here to watch a movie, I looked out for my bike in the huge motorcycle parking which was almost deserted the last time I saw it. A long queue of extremely close parked bikes fused my view as I patiently searched for the KKR number plate among dozens of KA registration numbers.

The only thing appreciative about my old secondhand Yamaha RX100 is that it is so old that Bangalore in Karnataka that time had KKR vehicle numbers, only to run out of all possible combinations that KA series came into being. Searching a unique number plate was probably the fastest way one could get to his bike in the long *Paras Cinema* parking.

Scanning the queue of number plates twice yielded no results, other than just convincing me that the bike was gone. Gone with the keys still in my pocket, for this KKR 6686 was a bike that could be ignited to life with any straight key...or even a piece of metal in that case.

I took out my cell phone, overlooked the bulk of missed calls and messages rotted into it, and called the contact Raghu.

"Where are you?" I fired rightaway.

"Hostel..."

"You bastard! What are you doing there? You took the bike too... I don't know... Come here fast and pick me up... Fast!" I shouted before he could say a word more.

"Hah…so you woke up finally! We tried waking you before leaving, but you refused. Now I'm in the hostel, it's too far *yar*…come yourself." Raghu's voice grunted through the microphone.

"What!! When did I refuse? And what come yourself? Come to *Paras Cinema* now or send someone with the bike… Its almost 10.30 *yar*… There won't be any buses too…".

After a syncing pause he replied, "Okay I'll come. Wait for sometime. Be there at the parking…".

"Cool. Come soon. Bye." I sighed.

As I found a moment of peace, I spotted a SBI ATM staircase which gave a clear view of the parking lot. Though I was famished, I just bought two Wills Navy-Cut cigarettes from a paan-shop and sat on the stairs.

I lit a cigarette and took the first drag, again pondering how I slept so deep that I didn't remember refusing Raghu to go along with him, the smoke went down my throat and into the lungs, and the feel of it suddenly bought back all the retentions of the last night that I was trying to recall for so long.

Ironically, the smoke cleared the air.

Yesterday night, Raghu, Sandy and I had come to this place that Raghu loves to call nothing else than 'Priya's home', and expects us to call that too.

Celebrating the end of our theory exams on the very same day, or searching a reason perhaps, we decided to come to 'Priya's home' and fly… Well virtually fly by smoking weed that is.

Raghu being a year senior to first-years Sandy and me, had known this place for quite long, and decided to bring two of his trustworthy friends, actually too trustworthy to tag along with him to his confidential place, to smoke marijuana i.e. weed, that he claims is the best and purest available in the whole of Bangalore city.

"You go to upscale pubs, find the best of nightlife or catch the best dealer roaming in Bangalore, I bet you'll never get weed better than this almost rundown building in the whole city, and the prices will be amazingly low only for us..." I remember him saying as we reached the small building into the busy streets of Old-Bangalore area, tripling on the already troubled bike.

"Come, we'll park the bike at a nearby theatre, as we are going to spend the night here." He declared with a wide smile as Sandy and I suddenly looked at him jaw-dropped, "Raghu, you kidding? Spend the night? Here?" I asked.

"Ya! You think we have come here for a couple of smokes? At least a good amount of weed until I'm completely out and a long sleep after that. Hitting the road after this can land us in a lot of trouble you know... Those 'don't drink and drive' cops are all over the place man.. And don't worry, I know the place very well." He said looking at the depressingly dark structure of the old building.

"Ya, you are right! *Don't drink and drive - 'Smoke weed and fly!'*" Sandy uttered with a thrill suddenly sounding hyper exited. I knew he was too happy. This was his dream come true. For a habitual smoker who loved the timely high of nicotine, a major stint with pure weed was all he lived for.

But I was most uncertain about myself, never ever even smelled marijuana leaf and not even too interested in doing so, I doubted my endurance amongst these weed fanatics. However Raghu was a man trusted, little did I knew that weed would make me forget myself for while and put me to sleep for twenty hours straight. What ground di others stood?

I smiled when I recaptured the other astonishments I went throug that single night. How people acknowledged Raghu's presence at that weary place or 'Priya's home' to be precise, the thrill in Sandy's voice when he found the weed effect so pure, the comfort with which Raghu took long drags and formed thick smoke rings. How smoke filled the room, the blur in my vision and the sudden heaviness I felt in my guts as I took the first drag of weed into myself, which later transformed into many drags, and a feeling of literally flying which never seemed to come down…and a vision which cleared only minutes ago.

My thoughts wandered further deep, I thought of Sandy, how the freak talked to me on our first day at Bangalore College of Engineering, the kind of audacious guy he really is, the way Raghu became such a good friend to me in spite of very few people he really counts as friends.

My six months into this college started with a roar, I thought of the remaining three years I'd spend here and thought about good days and good times to come and go.

Thinking of all this, I found myself smiling. Had I known about my fate and the puppet show of destiny better, and had I foreseen the future exactly a year from today, I wouldn't have smiled… I would have panicked and run.

But obviously I don't know that now. Or as a matter of fact, nobody has foreknown the lows and highs he has to go through, otherwise life was nothing but a meager run-and-chase game.

As the weed hangover took me deeper into thinking awful *gyaan* and I kept mooning on, a voice jerked my senses and Raghu appeared from nowhere, "*Hey!* Come let's go, I was looking for you near the parking." he said with a smile as always on is face.

"Oh hi, ya lets go. What took you so long? It's quite late." I said noticing 11.20 in my watch.

"Same old traffic on Hosur Road" he said and just when we reached the bike, he again turned, "Hey, I'll go see Priya once, you be here, I'il just come."

"C'mon, not now please, it's already very late. We'll come some other time" I said pulling his sleeve, "Here, I got a cigi for you." I offered him the remaining cigarette I had bought.

"Hmm... Ok, for the cigi this time. I'll come sometime else." he said while looking into the narrow alley that led to 'Priya's home' and got on the bike. I hopped on the pillion seat...and my beloved old rusty Yamaha roared to life.

"Did you see her? Was she there when you left?" Raghu asked me riding through the amuck night traffic in Bangalore. Honking and overtaking large trailers made us both inaudible.

"Ya, I did see her. She was the one who woke me up. It was kinda creepy *yar*, to get up alone at that place, that too in that claustrophobic room." I shouted leaning over him, to make the voice pass his helmet.

"I told that you refused to come along, you were too sleepy that time. And don't be a pussy... What makes you scared of that place?" He asked huffing out a laugh.

"Nothing. It's just that I was new there..." I said murmuring more to myself.

Well, anyone except the great Raghuveer Mishra would abstain from places like these. Or at least have a hint of guilt when he finds himself there at 10 pm, sleeping his heads off for almost a day, shirtless on a smelly bed which has seen thousands of beefy men bang prostitutes and calm their desires.

Yes, the building we insanely call 'Priya's home' is actually a brothel.

It houses six prostitutes and their pimp. Sandy, Raghu and I went there to do nothing more than just hire a room and go high on the amazing marijuana they sell, but that's not all for Raghu.

The only time I saw a flicker of tear in this emotionally-cold money driven human called Raghu was when he heard the situations that turn a young innocent village girl into a prostitute, or to be precise, when he heard the tale that forced 18-year-old Priya, the prostitute Neelam as most people know her, into what she is today.

Genuine or not, but that very moment I know Raghu had decided one *karma* he has to do in his life.

I know there will be a day when Raghuveer Mishra gets Neelam out of those dark lanes, out under the blue sky, at least a day before he himself gets chucked out of this world.

The fierce passion is blatant by a look in his eyes.

Empathizing with a prostitute was crazy. But I know Raghu can't help it. *Coz* Love is blind...and ruthless too.

Get Set…
We Met

The smell of Maggi noodles filled room no. 206, the room Sandy and I share at the BCE Boys Hostel. I idly walked around the dorm gallery, uncluttering my mind from the long list of Physics experiments I mugged an hour ago. Feeling the early dawn breeze from the window, I tried to rearrange the formulae list into my head and concentrated on each of them, hoping to recall it in the examination hall.

"So you done with it?", I asked Sandy as I entered the room, he crouched on the floor stirring the hot Maggi pan.

"Ya almost, it still not completely soft I guess" he replied slipping a single noodle from the pan into his mouth.

"What's not soft? I'm not asking you about that Maggi damn it! You done with the practical exam preparations?" I exclaimed and tossed his experiment handouts towards him.

"Oh, tomorrows physics practical? Ya, I read first six experiments, after eating I'll do the rest.", he said while tossing the notes back to the bed.

"Hey, its 4.40 in the morning, so you can't call it tomorrow. Now the exam is today! You still have nine of them remaining, the last ones are tough *yar*, so do it fast." I said as he raised the Maggi pan from the electric heater and kept it on the bed.

"Eat the Maggi you misery mouth…" he said with disgust.

"Roll number 92", the lab assistant howled. I entered the room an headed straight to the external examiner's table handling him my flims Hall Ticket. "Hmm… 92. Pick a chit from the box", he said with voice so deep that I thought he had a radio transistor forcibly shove down his throat. I picked a chit from the empty chalk box which wa now utilized into a lottery box and passed it to the transistor.

Chit system, also called as lottery system, is a method widely use to conduct practical examinations in engineering colleges. It is th best way the sadistic University could think of, to make the studen study all the experiments in the syllabus, even though he has to answe only one of them in the exam.

"Hmm… 16th one. Fermi Energy… Write the procedure and sta the experiment. The expected value is 6.728 eV, correct to two decim places…", the transistor groaned with a louder volume.

Taking the plain sheet from him, I whined that out of all the sixtee experiments, I got the last one, the most difficult one. Cursing m luck, I sat on the bench to write the procedure I least studied, unlik others that I had read atleast twice. Only this one I took for grante thinking that out of all sixteen, my luck wasn't exclusively hand crafte in hell to land up on the most difficult one.

But here I was, having a blind date with 1/16th of probabilit wondering now what happens to the rest fifteen that I perfected. Courte the luck… or whatever shit you call it.

Sitting dejected, as I struggled to finish the procedure writing, hand signalled Sandy sitting at the other corner of the room, askir him which number had he got. One and six, he showed one-by-or with his fingers. One and six, 16! I decoded.

Ok, so Sandeep aka Sandy, who barely read the first ones, had landed up with the toughest of em all. But a wide smile while showing those numbers, one and six, disturbed me further.

Was he so happy to get the sixteenth one? Or did he get seventh one and I misread it? Or was he just not bothered about the practicals?

With a procedure, tabular column and circuit diagram infested with errors, I moved to the experiment table hoping for a miracle to happen and all circuits and formulas working up to the magical number 6.728.

After an hour long struggle, 5.47, the calculator flashed. I reconnected the circuit, again calculated the values and reapplied the formula. 5.469, the calculator flashed happily, unaware of my tormented state.

After a long trial of peeping around and asking others, and getting looks of contempt as if I just asked them to drop their pants, I decided to surrender to the reality rather than still waiting for some magical powers to arrive.

Thrusting the paper into lab assistant's hand, or lab ass as they are popularly known, I moved out of the complexities of Fermi energy and the negative energy of the huge Physics Lab, and went to the Sutta-point, a place where everyone finds serenity, or at least I do.

The Five Star Restaurant, or Sutta-point as most hostellers call it, is a *dhaba* just off BCE Campus with a small seating area, partially under a concrete roof and a plastic shed.

The man at the shop, Manju-bhai, is a short and obese South-Indian who earns more-than-a-living by selling anything that is likely to attract the student's taste buds. From omelettes to ginger-tea, to making amazing chicken-rice, at least edible unlike the hostel-mess food, Sutta-point has it all, and most importantly it's got what I came here for, cigarettes.

"Two Navy-Cuts and a tea…", I sighed as I reached the glass top counter that had cheap pastries and biscuits displayed underneath.

"So, how are the exams going? When are you going home Ali?" Manju bhai asked while pulling two cigarettes out of the box.

"Theory papers were fine. Had a practical today, got fucked quite badly." I replied while wondering how Sandy had done.

"And when are you going home for vacations?" Manju bhai continued.

"Only after the Computer practicals now. That's after four days. I have KK Express tickets done, but am on the Waiting List. Around 200. Let's see..." I said picking up the tea cup and took a deepest drag I could manage.

A sudden ruffle in my hair abruptly chimney-ed out all the smoke off my nostrils. "How's it going baby?", Abdullah smirked.

I looked back and cold-shouldered him.

"You getting irritated? Oh my god! Save me. I'm frightened." He continued despite my snub.

"Fuck off! Do what you are here to do and get out of my sight..." I hurled after a pause, standing up and moving away from him.

"Hey Abdullah, come here and give me the stuff... fast!" Manju bhai called out. He took a couple of small tiffin boxes from Abdullah and sneaked a rolled bundle of rupee notes into his hand...like always.

Just when he was about to get on his bike and leave, he saw me standing out. Walking up to me, he got his sweaty negro face inches away from mine, "I'll get you one day..." he said looking straight into my eyes, and left.

I clenched my fist and thought we'd break into a fight.

If I have to confess, I got shit-scared.

"How was it? Which one did you get?", I asked Sandy waking him up from his afternoon nap as I reached the hostel room.

"Told you *na*? Fermi Energy, sixteenth", he said peeping out of his blanket.

"Which one did you get? How was it?" he continued.

"I too got Fermi Energy *yar*. It was too bad, I'll just pass. Got 5.47", I said kicking off my shoes.

"Why couldn't you do well? You studied all of them. Well, I easily got 6.73, that asshole examiner was quite impressed", he said going back into his blanket.

"What?? You got the value? How? You didn't even read that one.", I complained like a nag.

"Hey!! Who said I didn't read that one? Then how did I get the values? Actually after eating Maggi I was quite full, so I slept for a while, only to get up half-an-hour before the exam. It struck me that you had said the last ones are tough, so rather than panicking and doing all of them, I read the last two properly. I prepared for the worse and thankfully fished out one of those from the box. Hah! Relief.", he narrated his story which in short meant his luck was too good, or maybe mine was too bad.

"Oh, so you studied only eight and got through smoothly. Look at me, I left only one and got stuck on that.", I said while slipping into my bed. "Ok, I'll catch some sleep… Was up whole night." I said yawning.

I wondered that he managed to sleep the night before, read only eight out of sixteen experiments, and cakewalked the exam. While I stood up the whole night, read fifteen out of sixteen, and still let a lousy experiment screw my ass.

I cursed my luck further until sleep put me off in a minute. As always, sleeping cajoled all the pains.

"*All you touch and all you see... Is all your life will ever be...*", Raghu entered the room with Pink Floyd on his lips.

"Hey get up, it's almost midnight. Let's start studying...", he patted awkwardly curved Sandy's body dug deep in slumber. The way Sandy slept, babies don't sleep that well.

It was remarkable to see Sandy's endurance during examinations. They say examination days in an engineering course are something you will dread the rest of your life. A gloomy atmosphere prevails in the hostel. The lights never switch off. The faces become intense and distressed. Those who use to hum songs now mutter only physics formulae. Book stacks swap CD stacks, and magazines make way for old-question papers. All the heads seem to be down on books as if they are fixed.

When you get ten days of preparatory holidays to study 3600 pages of notes, plagued with an ever-expanding population of formulas, derivations and theories that only their inventors could understand, this seem to be the only way out to survive the onslaught.

As a result, for people like me, a reason called 'exam stress' turns into an easiest available opportunity to overcome the hurdles of your inner-conscience to take their first puff. Up goes tensity in smoke.

But then there are exceptions, Sandy was one of them. When everyone find themselves trapped in the night-before-the-exam jinx, and try to memorise impossible amounts of illogical sciences, Sandy roams in the deserted dorm gallery listening to Bob Dylan and Jimi Hendrix on his pod.

Around four hours of uninterrupted concentration is all the damn he gives to those attention hungry engineering books. 'Mug it a night before, vomit everything on the paper…forget it forever', is one of his theories.

"See, first nine are quite easy and finish them soon. Then we'll look at the rest eleven, I'll explain you those…" Raghu said as we sat cross legged on the bed… The room silent and our faces serious.

Rest of the night was filled with the smell of Maggi noodles, sound of whistling coffee maker, smoke from the smoldering cigarette, and yes, a little bit of studies. Only if a human mugging a two hundred line computer code is called studying.

The exam was dead easy. Again the Lab ass howled 'Roll no. 92', again I entered with a sweaty face, but not again got a difficult experiment. Or in that case no one gets into a 'God help me!' situation in the C Language Lab. The subject is easy when compared to other nightmares, so less people bother God and disturb Him from His morning sleep on this examination day. God is happy and so are we.

Adhering to my after-exam schedule, I went to the Sutta-point, to relieve a compressed chunk of computer codes clotted into my mind. To mix it up with the Navy-Cut smoke and release it from the chimney of my mouth.

"Hey Manju-bhai, change your shirt *yar*. It's become brown from its original white." Raghu entered as he picked one of the two cigarettes I bought. Somehow my second cigarette always ended up with him, I thought for a second.

"Why *yar* Raghu? None of the babes coming here will notice me. Look at me, so old I've become, and this tummy", Manju bhai said resting his palms on his rotund belly which was thankfully covered under the flimsy white t-shirt which he always wore. The big bold letters 'USA' on the shirt was something that ensured he was a true Indian, who else would use a US t-shirt as a spare one for his daily chores and carelessly let it go soiled.

"What's up?" Raghu asked letting go the conversation with Manju-bhai, "How was the Lab Exam?"

"Ya, it was pretty good. I got an easy one.", I promptly replied. "How was the your lab?"

"It was just ok *yar*. Only three people got final output out of all twenty." he said yawning.

"You?"

"What you?"

"The output. You got it?" I asked almost certain to get a negative answer.

"I was one of the three." he said reaching out for the tea.

"What!!...I mean…umm...hmm...hey that's amazing man", was all I could manage to say.

There are times when I try to figure out this person called Raghuveer Mishra. This moment was one of them. I looked at him as he chatted with Manju-bhai… the sounds of conversation going mute to me. How he tried and always succeeded to look at the cut-the-flab part of things bewildered me. There was a certainty in his aura… the certainty that he knew what was going around, the certainty that he could always see what lies beneath. Surrounded by people who have devoted their lives living someone else's lives, he wasn't one of them… He was him.

Of all the nerdy-comes-to-school and soda-glasses people stuffed into his class, I wondered how he managed to secure a seventh rank in the University when no one else could ever disturb a single-digit slot. When I was busy trying to forget the codes I read the night before, how he remembered them even after a year and taught me those with such a command. Doesn't his mind get clotted with them? I tried to reason, like always, only tried.

"Remember", Raghu tapped my nose with the stiff paper of a Railway-ticket, "Exams over. Now going home!" he said with exhilaration.

"Ya, but the tickets are waiting list. A week ago it was 200.", I said.

"And today 150", he said checking it in his cellphone.

"So, what are we gonna do now? The train is at 8.30 pm, only four hours left."

"Let's see...pack your bags. We'll go to the station first. I'll talk to the TT, there should be some way out.", he said gulping down the remaining tea.

This was the time of the year that Sandy spent with his parents, or rather spent at his home. Unable to sustain the emptiness of 'the rich life' and white uniformed butlers standing beside him even when he ate his breakfast, he usually joined some adventure trekking or mountaineering group and didn't return home for days.

I remember the last time we went to his sprawling palatial villa... The butlers welcomed us better than the Government welcomes foreign delegates. Even the college bag I carried was taken away by a butler obsessed with his plastic smile.

Seeing all varieties of Chicken and Mutton spread over the lunch table, I would have eaten enough to starve for four days straight, but with butlers standing just next to you and constantly gazing at your plate with curved lips that they were born with, I bet you can't let go the spoon-fork combination... I wonder how rich people eat.

"I hate it here man. Mom and dad don't have time to even see that I'm here with my friends, so they send these paid smiles.", he said persuading me to stop playing the X-Box in his room and leave the place, or the palace perhaps.

"Here, we'll take this to hostel. Now leave that", he said taking out a PSP from his wardrobe. For a second for which the closet opened, I saw heap of probably a million gadgets, all ignored.

"Whoa! Hey…oh my god...u have this? Never told me asshole." I reacted as if a nude Pamela Anderson rolled out of his wardrobe.

"Okay now hold this… we'll go", he said switching off the X-Box, I switched on the PSP.

All along the way, I wondered how one could never make out that this chap was in a pool of money. That happened everytime I visited his fort like home, the Sandy-*Qila*, I use to call it.

"Okay bye. Happy home-trip", I sarcastically said patting Sandy's back just when Raghu and I were about to leave for the railway station.

He murmured something to me which was possibly a strong abuse, those which include your seven generations in one word.

I let it go as today was the day he dreaded, his month long home-trip was about to start. For me it was something I longed for.

After killing an hour more, Raghu and I left for the station, hoping for some miracle to happen with the ticket.

'Never underestimate the power of stupid people in large groups' I had read this one-liner many times, but that day standing on Platform no. 3 of the Bangalore Railway Station, I was convinced beyond doubt that it was true.

Large hordes of people ran up and down the platform shouting something hoarsely that I didn't care to listen to, or maybe I was jealous of their determination, the determination and confidence that they would somehow struggle into the train which was about to leave in fifteen minutes. The struggle of the common man... That he will get what he wants... Come what may.

Raghu and I stood beside the flowing crowd towards the platform wall, hopes of a miracle being crushed to death in front of us.

"Hmm...don't panic...lets analyze the situation... What the fuck is going on here!" Raghu's voice that started calm suddenly rose into a wild shriek.

"All we can do is give it a try, let's join the crowd and look out for a bogey which is least crowded. The train moves in ten minutes, we can't accomplish anything standing here." I said picking up my backpack. This was probably the first time that Raghu kept silent and I was the one making sense.

"Ok, let's try. And hey, keep your wallet in the front pocket, or you'll never know when it is gone."

We joined the crowd, determined and confident that we won't be able to do anything here. The smell of sweat, struggle and persistency welcomed us. Suddenly I was not making any effort to move, the crowd just took me along. Just when I heard the whistle of the train, a hand clenched my wrist and pulled me out of that world.

"Whoa! Man...that was impossible", it was Raghu. That was all he said as he left my hand, we quietly watched the train chug along, people still running into it, and for the first time in my life, I missed a train.

"Let's get this ticket cancelled now. Huh, never expected this...", Raghu said after the train disappeared in the dark.

"Fuck! This can't be happening, I... I mean... what the fuck yar...!"

I stammered something that I knew was lame. People who say 'this can't be happening' long after it has happened are the lamest according to me.

The ticket we had thought so much about got cancelled at last, we strolled out of the station into the cool night-breeze of the city and got into a crowded BMTC bus which was heading towards Electronic City, having no choice but to see the empty hostel. "I have KK Express tickets done, but under Waiting List. Around 200. Let's see." I remembered telling Manju-bhai... the crowd of the bus seemed nothing.

"Aren't you people supposed to be gone by now? Everybody's left I think...", Manju-bhai said as he saw our sleepy faces next day morning at the Sutta-point.

"What to tell you Manju-bhai... the ticket was waiting and probably the whole of Bangalore wanted to get into that train yesterday..." Raghu said lighting a Navy-Cut.

"Hey, let's call Sandy and at least tell him that we're still here", I said taking out my phone.

In around half-an-hour, Sandy showed up, dressed in a night-suit, but sitting in a chauffeur-driven Honda CRV.

And then sitting on that ailing bench at the Sutta-point, we laughed till our guts ached, on our condition the night before, on how Raghu reacted when he saw the crowd, how I just sailed in that smelly swarm and how porters abused me...

"Hah, enough yar. Stop it now!" Sandy gasped as he collected air to breath. "What are you people gonna do now? When you going?"

"Don't know man. I'm gonna check air-tickets… What else is possible?" I asked myself.

"You'll try for tomorrow right? You think you can get tomorrow's ticket so easily?" Sandy said getting up. "I got to get home. Mom is there today… I have some work *yar*. I'll come in the evening."

Sandy left, me and Raghu kept sitting on the bench wondering what next. That was the day I truly felt free, completely redundant after a long time. All the strain and worries of examinations, college timings, studies, everything gone. "Fuck going home! I'm happy", I thought to myself.

After a heavy afternoon lunch, I was looking out of the room window wondering what to do about the tickets. The hostel was deserted, and a gallery which never slept finally took a month long nap. The black Honda CRV appeared again, the sharp light of sun shone on the bonnet. Sandy walked out, this time not in a night-suit.

In a minute the room door slammed open, "Hey sup?" he said entering.

I kept silent, and seeing me lying on the bed, he started laughing again, "Oh my God! Look at your condition. How will you get a train now?" he asked a question that he knew I couldn't answer. I too joined the laugh session, and the gallery was no more gloomy.

"Fuck you man! Get lost." I said huffing for air. "No *yar* I'm serious. What do we do now? Air tickets for tomorrow are a fuckin 10 grands…"

"We do nothing. Today night plans are set. Buffet at Empire Restaurant. Fuck you gotta try the mutton there… Well whatever... After eating all the food there, we go to smoke weeee…"

"No way… Go to hell! I'm not able to find a means of getting to Delhi anyhow and you expect me to smoke grass…not happening." I announced, maybe it was that weird night that terrified me more than all that I just blabbered.

"Now? Is it a happening now?" Sandy said reaching for his wallet and held out an envelope towards me.

Miracles do happen, you just need to recognize their form. It was a confirmed KK Express ticket for the next day. For the world it might be just a ticket, but for me, in that precise moment, it was the world.

"Wh…Wha...What is this? Oh my God! How?" I said trying to control myself from kissing his ugly face. I kissed the ticket instead.

"I told mom..." he said. "She asked where you people wanted to go, and then called up someone."

"Then?"

"Then what. Someone came home, some short bald fellow with a big paunch, I tell you he was such a joker. You know he…"

"Ok ok…continue! Don't tell me about that fellow *yar*…what the fuck? What happened next..." I interrupted.

"What what happened next? He just gave the envelope to mom, and after some regular buttering and flattering… he disappeared."

"Fuck man! How did she get it done? That too instantly"

"Hey chuck it *yar*…you got the tickets no?"

"Ya I got the tickets… That's ok…but I mean…how to thank you…You actually…"

"Cut the crap you ass! What's wrong with you? Get off that mode."

"But…you don't know it was impossible to…"

"Now this guy's lost it!" he put an abrupt end to the melancholic drama and went to the loo.

Similar excitement but much less of an emotional drama followed when Raghu saw the ticket. Suddenly Sandy became everyone's hero.

If I didn't have a limited capacity to stuff food into myself, or if science had invented a detachable spare plastic stomach, Empire Restaurant would have closed down long before. For ninetynine bucks, the buffet it offered had everything possible to derive out of chicken and mutton, and something sweet which tasted like *kheer,* I hate it when South-Indian restaurants try their hand at classical delicacies. Chicken and mutton might be good, but *kheer* is something only mothers can cook.

"See I'm telling you, you've hogged enough…or you'll burst *yar*! Let's get out of here now" I shook Sandy who was busy tearing a mutton piece so fiercely, I bet the lamb would be feeling the pain all over again.

"Whuff off…" he said with his mouth full.

The Yamaha RX100 had a tough time again. Three fat-asses strangulated it's throat as now the CRV was sent home, as now was the time no one in the world was suppose to know what these three souls are upto, as now was the time to *fly*.

We reached 'Priya's home' again, it was 10 pm into the night. From the parking in *Paras Cinema* to the SBI ATM staircase, everything hounded me and reminded me of that other night while I was busy ignoring the jitters. That was the first time I realised I really wanted marijuana - I wanted it desperately. I wanted it now.

"Hmm…hey let's not smoke in that crammed room this time. Just buy the stuff from here...we'll go to some open place…" I said hesitantly just when we were about to get into that narrow staircase. Raghu and Sandy looked at me and laughed.

"Relax, we won't leave you alone this time *yar*", Raghu said turning at Sandy.

"We're here only to smoke, remember? Nothing else… Chill, nobody will fuck you." Sandy chuckled and patted me on my back.

Jerking off Sandy's hand, I shouted in a rawest possible tone I could manage, "Shut the fuck up you two! I don't give a damn. I'm just not going into that *randi-khana*!".

For sometimes you wish that words could've been taken back, but Raghu always had a way out. I thought the worst he could do was a straight square punch flat on my face, but he managed to do something far more disturbing, he just smiled.

"Hey, sorry *yar*. You know I didn't mean it." I tried damage control. "I'm just..."

Before I could complete my pseudo talk, Raghu climbed up the stairs. "Wait there, I'll come." he shouted back... and a thousand words were left unsaid.

"Hey... It's okay *yar*. I just blabbered something. We'll go there itself... I'm telling no... Please..." I said to pay something in return... but all I could convince myself was the terrace.

So in the chilling night-breeze of Bangalore, we sat on the roof of a brothel, wrapped in smelly blankets used by men I didn't wanted to think about, rolling joints of one of an illegal drug. Drug that was when caught at airports even in a few grams, could lead to years behind bars, was lying in front of us, atleast half a kilogram.

'No pain no gain' as it is said, rolling weed joints is a tedious job. Small piece of a special paper, same as that in a cigarette, is taken and powdered weed leaves mixed with tobacco are rolled into it, a filter at the bottom completes it, and junkies call it a *joint.*

"Fifteen sixteen seventeen, now let's start?" Sandy asked as he counted the total number of joints the four us of made in ten minutes.

The junkie who got the weed for us and worked as a middleman in the area, decided to join us. He was a lean, dark and a gaunt South-Indian, we didn't know each other's language and as they say 'Speak the language of love and you can travel the world', we spoke the language of 'Weed'. His intense eyes behind those thick eyebrows told only one thing – 'Let's get high kids!'

"Name Name *nam*?" Raghu asked him.

"Prabhumasulu" he said staring at us with those dozy eyes, expecting smiles of acceptance.

We smiled and so did he, his beetle-red teeth showed clearly out of the thick grey stubble which covered most of his face.

The first few drags dried my throat like a rain deprived crop field, and as the amazing grass showed its wonder, I was elevated to a different world. Finally, the true kick was here.

While the pure weed surely did its job on Sandy and me, and even Raghu, Prabhumasulu smoked joints like Navy-Cut cigarettes, thick smoke rings furiously emerged from his mouth while the stick remained between his lips. He breathed marijuana.

The next time I looked down, his busy hands had completed converting the half-a-kilo heap of grass into joints, atleast a hundred of them.

"He is ready to make money, now he'll sell these to foreigners and customers till early morning", Raghu said pointing at the plastic bag stuffed with joints.

I nodded.

"You know what is that stuff he has mixed with the pure weed?", Raghu continued.

I noticed another heap of dry powder kept aside the bag.

"Ya I know, that's tobacco." I said in a drowsy voice, answering someone's questions is the worst spoiler that can happen to a great kick.

"Oh that's tobacco is it? Thanks for telling me *yar*... That's dried cowdung you ass!", Raghu said smelling a pinch of the remaining powder.

Before my reaction time, which was further delayed due to the weed effect, could take place, Raghu again struck, "Hey chill! That's only for those foreigners and amateurs, we get only the pure stuff."

I again leaned back on the terrace wall, the kick returned.

Prabhumasulu, who didn't understand a word of our conversation, suddenly got up to leave. The vigour in his body was the same as when he started the weed-session, infact it wasn't a session at all for him, weed joints for him was like Navy-Cuts to me. With the same eerie smile, he bid us good bye and passed me a couple of joints from the packet. I knew what they had in them and tossed them out from the wall behind me. 'What happens to those *firangs* who don't know that?' I thought for a moment.

Next thing I knew was harsh sunlight piercing me, same dryness donned my throat and same sound of bustling traffic bought me to life, a mosquito coil smouldered in front of me and reminded me of yesterday night's smokes. The only difference was that this time I wasn't trapped in a wooden room at 'Priya's home', but lying freely on the terrace of it, under the shining white sky.

I slowly walked down the narrow staircase reeling under a very familiar feeling, opting not to go into any of the rooms to search for two of my friends, I decided to go down and call Sandy on his cell.

"I'm standing down. It's 8 o clock. Come fast." I said still trying to adapt my sleepy eyes to the morning brightness.

By the time I bought two Navy-Cuts from a paan-shop and lighted the first one, sleepy figures of Raghu and Sandy emerged from the weary doorway of the building.

"Walk fast you two! We have to reach the hostel Raghu!" I called out.

"Hmm…" Raghu grunted and took one cigarette from my hand. Yet again, I thought.

Once again Sandy went *home* and I returned to the hostel room… the train was at 7 pm in the evening.

It was around 11 am when something struck me and I instantly got up from my bed.

"Hey I'll have to go somewhere. I'll come in an hour" I told Raghu and slammed the door behind me. I picked up the bike and sped off.

I rode the bike looking around for any nursing home or hospital in the area… a few kilometers away I found one.

'A.M. Nursing Home' the semi-circular display board read.

'Whatever Nursing Home!' I thought to myself, as all I had to do was get a tetanus injection, and any small place with a couple of white-coats employed would have been enough for that.

I walked in unaware of the world that the next few moments held in them… And the freaky story of my life that they would kick off from now on.

The same creepy hospital smell welcomed me. A smell that personified the emptiness of life, the silence of it.

"Sister, where to go for a TT syringe?" I asked a nurse who looked awful enough to be comfortably called a sister.

"Hmm… Go to that room sir. I'll come." She said something that raised doubts in my mind. 'My sick brain!' I thought in disgust.

I sat in that small room just when the same 'sister' entered with a loaded syringe in her hand.

Now I'm not particularly phobic to getting a shot or whatever, but looking at it while it slowly pierces my skin shudders me. I raised the sleeve of my shirt and looked the other side, anticipating a prick into the upper end of my hand.

"Sir, please sit there" she said with a smile as I suddenly turned to her. Her direction was at the stretcher-bed kept at the corner.

"There? Umm… I mean… Why there sister?" I asked hesitantly, again raising my sleeve till the maximum.

"It'll be on the butt sir. TT injection should not be on the hand. It forms a clot. Now lie there upside down… Fast please. Other patients are waiting too."

By the time I thought of a way to dissuade her and searched for correct words, I found myself already lying on the stretcher with a piece of my ass opened to a stranger I met minutes ago.

"Over sir. It's done. You can get down." She said pressing a cold cotton on the newly pierced area of my modesty.

The embarrassment I suffered in the past two minutes was by now largely visible on my face. But I found my own condolence in the fact that only a nurse got to see the color of my underpants and whatever was visible through the small sliding it had suffered, and she was least bothered about it.

Just when I got down and let out a sigh of relief, I suffered a shock that would've surely given me a cardiac-arrest or whatever deadlier… but luckily it didn't.

A girl stood just in front of me, the 'sister' nurse hurriedly went past her out of the room, I blankly stared at her as if I was witnessing a extra-terrestrial, the pressure of my thumb died and the cotton dropped, suddenly I realised she had seen the entire ordeal I went through. I too rushed out of the room avoiding a direct look in her eyes.

By the time I gulped-down four glasses of water and reached the payment counter, to my utter embarrassment, I saw her again, this time sitting at the payments collection counter.

I eyed her from a distant view that I could get, her pink t-shirt and blue jeans was the brightest thing in the lifeless hospital. A white surgeon's coat hung behind her chair.

'Whoa! She's beautiful! Who is she? What is she doing here? And most importantly, what was she doing in that room?' a million such thoughts rushed into my head.

I walked towards the payments counter and placed my token in front of her.

"Token 10. TT syringe" I said looking down, trying hard not to let her recognize me.

"Name" she said looking straight at me.

Now till this day, I had seen numerous beautiful girls and eyed and ogled them in ways that would make even dogs look for cover. But for the first time in my life I realised, voice is something that really defines a girl's beauty, and that was the most beautiful voice I'd ever heard. Though *beautiful voice* may be grammatically incorrect, but that is what it was – *beautiful.*

"May I have your name please?" I was suddenly jerked into reality.

"Hmm… Ya… Ali. It's Ali" I said trying hard not to stammer and recollected myself. "Ali! Don't be a dumb woman-deprived desperate asshole. Listen and respond!" I ordered myself.

"Age?"

"20"

"Any allergies?"

"No"

"Thirty rupees" she said as the bill printed.

"Ya… here you are." I held out a five-hundred rupee note, the only money I had with me.

"*Naah…* Change. Get change." she said getting up from the chair and making way for the 'sister' nurse. I knew she was just passing time sitting there, she couldn't be a cashier. Somehow I could feel that she was someone there.

"I don't have any change sir. Go get it please." the new nurse played the same tape, but in a more snobbish tone this time.

I couldn't see *her* anywhere now, and this time consuming hospital visit was getting over me, the 'sister' nurse's polite snub added to the situation and at last it got me triggered.

"What the hell? You got so many payments going on here and you say you don't have any change in that drawer *huh*? Whom are you trying to fool? Just do your job no!" I shouted in a rather high-pitched tone, only to attract a few placid glances from the patients waiting in the lobby. Hospitals are always dead.

"But I told you I don't have any!" the nurse replied without much of a concern.

'What do I do now? Bitch!' I murmured to myself and turned away from the counter suddenly finding *her* standing just in front of me, again the same way.

"Here's your 470 bucks. Many fools come here and shout for petty reasons like change every single day, but only a few have the common-sense to go outside and find it in surrounding shops. But no fretting, I do the job for them. Now collect your bill from the counter and please get lost if you're done..." her words shamed me enough for the words in my mouth to go for a six.

Without saying anything, I pulled the notes from her hand looking straight into her deep black eyes.

And just like that, on a dull Bangalore afternoon, in sheer hospital creepiness, looking into each other's eyes...*we met.*

The Slumdog

It was good to be in the train at last, seeing Bangalore dissolve in darkness as the train moved further induced a satisfaction, a pacifier to the fact that we had missed the same train a day ago.

"Fuck! I found one… Look at her. She's kinda hot you can say…" Raghu said with his eyes fixed on a girl standing near the doorway, thankfully looking the other side.

I carefully examined her before coming up with any of my invaluable ratings. Her face could barely be seen but none of us wanted to see that either, her tight body hugging top gave a good embossment of the stuff she wore inside… and the jeans under it was so tight that I wondered how she had got into that. Was it stitched directly on her body? Or was she born wearing those?

"*Naah*… hotbod but cheap. Probably one from Sandy's shut-the-face-fuck-the-base category.", my ratings sounded something like that… and I was calling her cheap.

"Hey!! You forget it *yar*… I just asked how is she and you even fucked her in your thoughts. Sorry to disturb you, you continue reading your book..."

Suddenly while reading I felt a twitch under me which reminded me of the morning tetanus shot, and almost instantly reminded me of a voice that was beautiful.

"Hey you know I saw a girl today!" I said turning to Raghu the very next moment.

"Saw a girl means what? See I understand you are a bit, hmm… let's just say hyper-sexual and all that, but how come even seeing a girl is that big a deal now?"

"What hyper-sexual? I mean I met a girl. A very beautiful girl... Very beautiful" I said again diving into thought.

"Where?"

"At a nursing home. I went there for a tetanus shot."

"Why you always keep your health check-up and all complete before going to Delhi? You always get some injection or the other. What's the reason *yar*?" Raghu was interested more in the not-so-beautiful part. I was indeed happy that the conversation took another turn as I won't have to narrate all the embarrassment and humiliation I had to go through, as till now I gleefully told myself that I *met* that girl.

"Hmm... Why I keep a health check-up update? That's because I'm a member of the Delhi Cycling Club. I've told this to you before too." I replied after abruptly coming out of the beautiful voice thought.

"Cycle races? Fuck *yar*! That's so lame. How can some lousy cycle race by some lousy cycling club make you take all that pain? I've never seen you interested in any sports either. Just don't understand your crazy funda. What is it?"

The question suddenly shot me in the head. He was right, why did some petty cycling club got me so involved? I have never even participated in a race. Sports were the last thing I wanted to do before death. Then why? Though I knew the answer to this question, I always kept it to myself and let all the people around me come to awful conclusions about my insanity.

"Hey what you thinking now? Let's go near the doorway for a sutta... Hold this..." Raghu said passing me a Navy-Cuts' box. The question he had asked started hounding me now. None but I knew the answer behind it.

Get medical check-ups done everytime, submit the bills of your check-ups, and renew your membership. Why was I so much into it when late-submission or even no submission of college assignments and files didn't bother me to that extent?

We stood near the doorway of the coverage, the dry wind passing through my hair making them go wild. Raghu watched out for a Railway cop while I lit two Navy-Cuts, the train cut through the greens with vengeance, I took the first puff and felt the smoke…

"The reason behind that is too weird Raghu. I'll tell you, but I doubt if you would be able to understand…" I said looking at the smoldering cigarette tip, impulsively driven by the frustration to let out the heap of past that rested in my head.

"Hey… It's okay. Don't tell me if you don't want to. I just asked." Raghu said, wondering what suddenly made me so serious about his small question.

"No… I'll tell you. I don't give a shit about cycling. I do it to because I miss a friend I had. A friend…" deep thoughts and pictures surrounded my mind, Raghu kept silent, the guy knew when he had to, and those days of my life started crossing my mind.

"When we were kids… that is Gopal and I. He used to stay in a slum and I in the apartment buildings adjoining the slum area. Basically, he was a poor slum kid and I, a rich one."

Raghu silently saw me with 'what is he saying?' expression on his face.

"I was reminiscing more to myself…" I said looking at him, "Let me start somewhere in the beginning…"

I tried hard to remember the first few days of my childhood when I first met Gopal.

"Consider there are two kids... hmmm... one is a sorry-face dumb rich kid and the other, a poor and smart tough slum kid."

"So..." Raghu said with raised eyebrows.

"I still remember my real self when I was a kid, downright introvert, turning eyes inward for anything referred to me and getting bullied by every single guy around... this is all those days were about."

"I can't remark any single point in my childhood that something special or extraordinary happened, every day was a photocopy of a photocopy of a photocopy and so on. But a day came that was different."

A constable came and stood near us and Raghu instantly slipped the Navy-Cuts' pack into his pocket. I continued...

"That was the day when I met this guy called Gopal. I can't exactly recall the moment... Maybe he was all alone getting bored in the neighboring children's park when he approached me, as I sat there everyday blankly looking at other kids play and wishing I had been the one holding the bat and hitting one six after another, getting pats on my back from every jealous kid. Wishful thinking is the sport I've always played... Not cycling.

Gopal always used to wear those khaki ultra-mini knickers and shrunk tight shirts that surely used to come to him from some monthly charity given out to slum people. Yes, Gopal was poorer than the poor, he stayed in one of the thousands of slums covering every single piece of land adjoining the apartments where the rich lived.

When I belonged to the same community of rich kids, I never found a single friend in the park that was exclusively made for them.

Till the day I met Gopal...

While I was never ever too much of a best-friend and all that for him, but for me, a private school going self-absorbed snob, the time with him meant the world.

He was kept away from the cricket match that went on in the park, for he used to hit a six on every single ball and make rich kids run for the ball, and soon run out of breath. Or maybe the partial reason was his rugged clothes and typical 'poor-kid' looks.

His tall, sun-tanned and thin framework depicted the perfect breed that the mother's of rich-kids will advise their children to stay away from.

Gopal and I frequently used to sneak into Delhi Cycling Club. Amongst the thriving crowd we both used to sit and watch state-level players dressed like superman, riding fashionable cycles.

"I'll also be a cycling champion when I'll grow up Ali... You'll come to see my races no?" Gopal used to say looking at the cycle track with desirable eyes.

Suddenly one day Gopal came running and told me that he was being shifted to some quarters constructed by the Government for slum-dwellers, he was happy and I wondered if he was really going. And then I never saw him again, we parted as casually as we met.

"But you know what Raghu? Gopal was not a normal kid... He had some serious mental disorder... He used to get froth-fits and epilepsy-attacks every fortnight... And his parents, who were too poor to even think of the expensive medication, used to just tie his limbs to the wooden cot until his maddening hysteria and screaming due to the seizures rested... His mind was slowly approaching disability... But the smile on his face hid behind all the troubles of the lost childhood he lived. We both knew that he wouldn't always be the same. But we never discussed that...we just lived the moment."

"Eventually I was sent to boarding school in Bangalore. I stayed away from home, made friends, good and bad friendships came and went, but Gopal was one person who left his mark on me."

"There was a part in me that day-in-day-out just thought of Gopal. I was still that dumb sorry-faced rich kid, but Gopal taught me how to live life. How to make good friends and better foes...and be justified to both. How to hit back when you get hit, and bend the finger that points in your face."

"I still insanely go to that cycle-club to reminisce those days. My eyes still wander for him. I still find myself sitting in the crowd but not with Gopal beside me. I might be an emotional fool... and if I am, I wish I had never met him."

By now I could effortlessly visualize Gopal's face clearly in front of me. Raghu became the first person to know the reason behind my strange cycling whim. I jerked myself to the present, it was dark by now and the train slowed down as it approached some station.

"I told you *na*... You'll find it crazy." I said smiling at Raghu.

Raghu stared at me expressionlessly, "You are not as bad as you seem to be..." he murmured to himself.

I could see Raghu was baffled to know the depth behind what he till now dismissed as just another crazy habit of mine, "Hey let's get down here... See, that girl again!" he said as the train stopped at the station, trying hard to avoid the situation.

Days at home were in complete contrast to those in the hostel. Everytime I reached home with long locks and a small patch of beard over the chin which made mom think that I still hadn't learnt to shave properly. But nevertheless, the hair strands that took almost a year to grow were ruthlessly chopped off by the local barber in no less than a minute, I was told to shave properly, and to top it all, the prescribed specs that I had abandoned a long time ago were again fixed on my face, 'put them on or your eye-power will increase Ali' mom would say... which actually meant – no more arguments, shut your mouth and wear your specs all the time, you look like a good boy in them.

Short side parted hair, clean shaven face and reading glasses, I avoided periodic shocks by looking into the mirror, as it mercilessly reflected the real me, and I looked like shit.

It was a breezy morning and I came to the terrace with earphones on. My eyes wandered to the large glass covered shopping-mall and a shudder erupted deep within me, it suddenly rushed to my mind with a view of those thousands of slums built over that same area some six years ago. In one of those slums Gopal had spent his childhood, I couldn't understand why my mind failed to get over his thoughts, 'Fuck this place! When will I get back to Bangalore?' I asked myself.

Bangalore.

Night before the internal exams was bad, Majors do stir a little in our bowels and we somehow bring our ass to study at least a week in advance, but internal exams have this very complicated but comforting 'chill! You can perform better next time' feel induced in them, obviously just a feel.

The college conducted three internal exams, out of which only two are considered for the Majors. Sandy and I were easy prey to the nonexistent feel - 'Let's screw tomorrow's internal, we'll rock the other two' that we used to coax ourselves with... and would eventually end up screwing all three and rocking none.

This was the night before the third and the final internal and I had just realised that we'll-rock-the-next-one concept had failed to apply itself.

I woke up from my afternoon nap at around 11 pm. Realizing my nap had turned into a complete six hour sleep, I got panicked. I straightaway picked the fat Electronics book kept aside and marked the portions which was to come in tomorrow's exam, I realised I would have saved time marking the ones that were not coming. I flicked through the bulk of pages and saw hundreds of circuit-diagrams, derivations and what-was-that! stuff pass through front of me, all of it shouting and mocking towards me – "Let's see if you can cram all of me into your head in one night straight!"

I picked a Navy-Cut from under the pillow and walked out to the dorm-gallery hungry for fresh air, and cigarette smoke.

"Get up soon you ass! There's so much to study!" I shouted and shook Sandy. He slept on the other bed dug deep under his blanket. I pulled the blanket off him, only to find his boxer-clad naked body. 'Shit!' I dropped the blanket and barged out.

"You woke up? So how's the syllabus?" I re-entered the room after a few minutes, Sandy now sat cross-legged on the bed with the Electronics book resting directly under his gaze.

"Hey! I'm talking to you! How's the syllabus?" I again asked Sandy as he kept silent and didn't move, almost like a statue.

A minute went by when he suddenly erupted, "I dunno man… I dunno man… If you see this shit! Where does one start in this?"

Now this was something, for the first time I saw Sandy let pressure successfully climb over him, his reaction shattered even the tit-bits of some confidence that I had somehow managed.

"Really? Is it so damn big?" I asked again.

"Fuck the shut up! I'll kill you or kill myself by smashing my head against this book. Now stop doing this really-really and study!"

"Really!" I laughed him off and tossed the book aside and dropped myself on the bed.

Till now I had always known that ordinary things, when prefixed with the word 'blue', became great things, be it blue-film, blue-magazine or blue-whatever. But for some strange reason, universities around the world decided not to keep it all that great by naming the test-books as 'blue-books'. So when we stood up all night and broke our heads off after that comfortable feel of internal exams faded, we sat in the test-hall and wrote all that we retained on this *blue-book.* Just for a flimsy blue cover on the top, a nice healthy empty notebook became blue-book. Black-book was what it should have been, for it always bought dark thoughts and depressions with it...

Sandy studied for some time and I rightaway slept, quoting the logic "a human brain can't practically be taught all that in one single night", but as usual, for both of us none of the internals rocked and all of them screwed our asses. Black-book tag was further justified, every single time.

"Coming to Café Mocha?" Sandy finally spoke after keeping silent all the while I repeatedly asked him how he fared in the internal-test.

"Hey I asked you at least ten times and this is what... Whatever... Chuck it... Why Café Mocha now?"

"You coming or not? Answer fast or I'll go"

"*Naah*... You go yar. I don't feel like coming."

"You'll come. I'll fuel up and pay the bill too."

"No it's not about that... I just don't wanna go." *Obviously it was about that.*

"I'm telling you asshole, not asking you. Shut your mouth and come now." he said pulling me hard by the wrist. Actually the moment he asked - 'Coming to Café Mocha?', I knew I had no choice left but to go with him.

Sandy asked Raghu the same question, but his 'no' meant NO. I wish I too could be as firm on my ground as Raghu was at times, with friends like Sandy, anyone would.

"One hookah Nirvana... and two Expresso Blacks" Sandy told the waiter. The wall-clock touched 10 pm as we sat in the upscale coffee-pub in the Koramangala area. Blaring music played in the modified Lancers and Scorpios parked outside on the road-side. Rich brats and trying-to-be rich brats stood around in groups with Kingfisher cans in one hand and cigarettes in the other.

I fail to understand why these rich and spoilt brats can find only one way to show off their wealth, that is to stand around and hoot in sudden explosions of laughter, which became further terrifying when mixed with the shrieking music playing in their cars. They all have a strict dress code of shining leather jackets and leave doors and sometimes even the bonnets of their heavily stickered cars all open, for reasons even they don't know.

Thankfully they all liked booze-cigarette combo more than coffee-hookah combo and so had to stay out of the snugly, air-conditioned and 'babe-loaded' confines of Café Mocha. Babe-loaded it surely was, from short-skirted pretty *chinkis* to black nail-painted dusky after-eleven kinda lasses, all slightly head-banged to the 60's playing in the background and emitted thick smoke rings.

"Fuck! See the way that sonofabitch is feeling her... Man she's hot!" Sandy said looking through my shoulder. I slowly turned around to see a girl in ultra mini-skirts and a spaghetti top with a plunging necklines which made evident that the possessions she carried inside were hugely voluptuous, and a feast for voyeurs was she sat on her boyfriend's lap. The boyfriend, the guy that Sandy out of sheer jealousness rightaway declared as 'sonofabitch', was a typical breed of ubersexual males that were a recent crop in India, fair-skinned, clean-shaven, tight t-shirt with bulging muscles, weight where it should be, and a weighted wallet too. The *sonofabitch* deserved her, not two trying-to-be-ubersexual fat-ass engineering students.

Delhi and Mumbai had set the Café culture for rest of India to follow, their survival was dependent on the very crowd that they themselves invented. Ultra short-skirts and 'show-me-the-money-honey' babes were here, tinted car glasses were in. Whoa, India was changing and how!

Sandy and I sat there smoking hookah and sipping black-coffee like gays on their first-date, ogling all around trying to make most of our money, as usual Sandy spotted and I evaluated. And then suddenly everyone was requested to leave, the midnight deadline was here.

Sandy rode the bike back to the hostel, all along drag-racing with an unknown biker who came and stood next to us while we waited at a red-signal. This kind of scenario was common in Bangalore roads at night, a stranger may come and stand next to you on a red-signal, he revs up his bike and you get a signal of a race, when the green-light clicks, you start off as furiously as him and a fatal street-race begins. Sandy took these races dead seriously and be it pot-holes, leaking drains or one-ways, nothing could make him drop that accelerator. No cash-bets or prices were involved, all the madness was for one middle-finger that only the winner could flash. Sandy got to flash it back every single time. The rusty RX100 never let us down.

We reached the hostel room and even without removing my shoes, I dumped myself into bed and almost instantly dozed off. Though I was tired, the Mocha trip proved to be good, morning's bad internal-test seemed like a distant memory now.

The day was long and full of ups and downs, but thankfully and finally… it was over.

Talk. Text. Talk. Text

"One ticket… BCE" I told the bus-conductor trying hard to find a foothold in the crowded BMTC bus, cursing Sandy for roaming around somewhere with the RX and keeping his cell off all the while.

"*Yen* BCE… *Kaas kudho-appa… Aidhu rupaye*" the conductor rightaway replied in Kannada language, which meant – Don't just blabber BCE, give the money too, five rupees. My past five years in Bangalore had taught me the meaning of some basic local words, though I understood them, I never tried to speak them out to people, for all of them sounded the same and one could easily end up abusing someone just in an effort to greet him. I dreaded the image of me being thrashed in public.

The bus was moderately crowded and I was standing amongst a few men in the back side of it, holding on to the hanging handle, waiting for the BCE stop.

"Would you please get up… this is a ladies' seat" I heard a voice from somewhere in the front, it was familiar, it was *her*.

I cleared my way to the front, yes it was her. She was politely asking a couple of men sitting on ladies' seat to get up. She had her white coat resting on her arm, I looked at her lost in trance, the dim light of bus made her look dreamlike, the cold breeze out of the window slightly scattered her hair over her face. She was surreal.

"Get up would you?" she suddenly raised her voice towards the men and I recalled I too had been a victim of that short temper once.

I decided to stay away, I knew she'd create a scene. I loved to be an onlooker to ugly bus fights.

The guys, as I now looked at them and realised , were local goons, at least their appearance indicated they were. Big bush of curly hair and thick beard conveniently hid the real color of their skin, chains hanging out of every part of their clothing made me take two backward steps. They were the kind to whom I'd hurriedly handover all my cash, my cellphone, my watch and whatever that adds to my worth, even if they approached me just to ask time. But that was me, a tall dark lean ultra-submissive meek... She was brave, at least going by what she was doing now, either she was brave... or insane.

The guys kept on chatting amongst themselves and didn't move an inch, I expected that. She signalled the conductor to intervene but he looked the other side, I expected that.

Now the tension of the moment escalated, half the eyes in bus were fixed on the scene, and the guys, though they pretended to be unaware, knew that well.

"Hey... You gonna get up or not? You listening to me? I'm talking to YOU!" She erupted and suddenly the eyes fixed on her became twice in number. I knew they wouldn't move, and I knew she had landed herself in trouble amongst that unchivalrous male population of the bus.

I wished those guys were a little more human-looking in appearance rather than human-eating, and I could have tried my hand at some heroic stuff, but here the fairest of my chances were getting in the scene and losing my front two teeth right in the very first blow, I shuddered as my tongue ran over my teeth. Man, I loved them.

"One... NIMS" I heard her voice again and suddenly turned towards her from my journey of thoughts. She sat on the seat and the thug guys stood next to it. 'Whoa, it really happened. Amazing job!' I want to tell her.

She held out a ten rupee note while asking for a ticket to NIMS, National Institute of Mental Sciences. The wind made her long hair go amuck, pale moonlight shone one side of her face, I couldn't help but submerge into thoughts over and again, she was beautiful. And wise too... she held out money while talking to the conductor, unlike me.

It was 9 pm, why would she want to go to NIMS this late? Who was she? What does she do? Why was she there at that nursing home that day? I wanted to know her, wanted to talk to her, I wished I could've helped her somehow today.

The guys were still standing there and the frequency of their abrupt hoots of laughter was increasing every passing minute. Right next to her, they stood and passed comments and no one in the bus could raise a voice against them. I wondered how she sat so comfortably there looking gracefully out the window. She wasn't insane... she was brave.

NIMS was one stop before BCE. I somehow felt relieved as the bus approached NIMS, she'd go out and all will be okay, I thought to myself. As the bus slowed down at NIMS bus-stop and she got up to leave, the two thugs saw her and raced ahead to set themselves on the footboard of the bus.

'Fuck! They're gonna get down at her stop and do some shit!' For the first time my thought process was accurate, alert, quick and basically more self praise...

I had to do something, the bus almost stopped and the guys jumped out, I know they waited for her. She, totally unaware, started walking down the aisle towards the exit.

"Ali! Do something! Do you know what can happen to her? Do you see the dark outside? Do something... SOMETHING!!" A voice screamed in my head and I lunged forward and held her hand. Tight from the wrist. She stared back, I didn't leave. She wriggled, I didn't leave. My fist grew tighter as I looked at her struggling and shouting something that sounded like miles away... Suddenly my mind became the warm little concentrated centre of the world.

"Move the bus. Those guys got down for her" I mumbled to the conductor. He couldn't understand me but he understood what I was doing. The bus moved... Our eyes didn't.

"I'm sorry. Get down at the next stop. It wasn't safe here." I said looking at her delicate wrist that had reddened due to the pressure of my fist. Somehow feeling terrible to hurt her, I quietly moved back.

Till the BCE stop, I didn't look at her or lift my head. I didn't know whether she was mad at what I had done...or whether she even understood. Whatever, she too didn't speak a word. The oldies in the bus looked at each other and smiled, they knew what I had done. The conductor smiled at me. I ballooned up with pride...trying hard to curb a grin.

The bus stopped with a screech at the BCE stop, I saw her getting down. I approached the exit and felt an unease run through me. Would she talk to me? What would she say? What if I get dumbstruck?

I got down and the bus moved, leaving us both in the dense night at the deserted bus-stop. Even the dogs were too bored to get up and bark, I saw one of them opening an eye to make sure the bus hadn't dropped two aliens amongst them.

The quietness and numbness of the situation got over me, and without again even looking at her, I started walking down towards the long dimly lit road that led to the BCE Campus. Yes, I was dumb enough to do so, to not even strike a conversation with a girl whom I had just saved from getting raped. Well rape might be an exaggeration but doesn't it sound more dramatic that way?

I walked with restrained steps, not too fast – not too slow, conscious how I might be looking from behind. Shit! Why didn't I talk to her? Can I turn around and talk now? *Naah*… that'd look weird. So how am I ever gonna meet her then? Such million questions echoed in my head and then suddenly a voice put an abrupt end to all of them…

"Hey!" she called out from behind.

I turned around, she was standing at a distance from me, the dim street-light and the darkness around made her look larger than life… dreams included!

She was fair yet tanned, slim but not thin, she might have a world of anger on her surface, but her welled black eyes leaked out all the somberness. I could've managed more profound thoughts had the voice not repeated itself.

"Hey! You okay?" she waved at a lost me.

Again same situation struck – "Ali! Listen and respond!"

"Umm.. Ya.. I'm alright." I said walking towards her, again conscious steps.

"I think I've seen you somewhere. Recently… Hmm…" she said trying to place me.

"Nursing home. The change guy." I responded wondering whether I was such an ordinary face that people forgot me as soon as they saw me off.

"Oh! Ya… I knew it was you." She said pulling her ethnic jute bag, known more as *jhola,* and adjusting the coat on her hand.

I kept quiet.

"Hey I seriously thank you for what you did in the bus. I can't tell you the good you've done to me. Oh my god I acted so stupid..." There came the part I was desperately looking for. I jumped high in jubilation and repeatedly fisted the air... obviously in my thoughts.

"Hey it's okay..."

"No it's not just okay... I mean you acted so smart there. You just stopped me from getting down in front of all those people. That's so courageous."

'Courageous? Me?' By now I was rolling on the ground in fits of euphoria, thanks to my virtual world.

"And the way you held my hand... I would've almost slapped you... had I not sensed that there's something more than what it looks like..." she said and the words 'slapped you' got me straight up on the ground.

"Oh... I'm sorry for that. By the way, I know you'd have easily done that. You seem quite of that sort." For the first time I spoke one full sentence to her without stammering.

Sandy always said that how much ever of a smooth-talker you might be, if you don't stammer for the first time in front of a beautiful girl, then she isn't beautiful. How much ever I rubbished his weird and pervert theories, they all came back to me and proved themselves at most inappropriate of times.

"Quite of what sort?" She asked laughing. *Oh, so we are getting into a conversation here.*

"Quite of sort to shout at hooligans in a bus. And shout until they jump out of their seats. Hmmm... Then teach people how to get change, the hard way. And all this from just two times that I've seen you." I was speaking at last.

"Oh you still remember that! I'm sorry for whatever I uttered okay..." She said, unaware of the fact that I'll never forget that day, the day I saw her for the first time.

"It's okay…"

"But you too acted too dumb there… and I heard what you called that nurse okay." she said.

I kept quiet.

"Hah! It was a long day... It's pretty late I guess… I must get going now…"

I was still quiet. I was lost looking at her.

"Well… Hi… I'm Divya" she said stepping forward and offering a handshake.

"Ali" I said and held her hand, thankfully not by the wrist.

An awkward silence followed.

"You study in BCE?" she thankfully broke it.

"Hmm… Ya… Not sure about the studying part though."

"Oh ok… and which year?" she asked overlooking my terrible attempt at a joke.

"Third year… And you? You're a nurse right?"

"What!! What did you just say?? I'm what??" she exclaimed. The expressions on her face changed in a flash, as if I just farted in front of her… that too one of those noisy ones. One of those Sandy ones.

"No… I mean… I thought… You were a nurse or something…"

"Hey are you crazy?? What makes you think that??" she asked with a open-eyes look, a slight smile donned her face, sky's full-moon reflected in her watery eyes and strands of hair fell over her face. I wanted to hold them and set them apart, and I did so, courtesy my thoughts.

I returned to the moment. "Umm… That day at the nursing home… and today at NIMS. You are always at hospitals… So I thought you were a…"

"Hey stop it! I'm not a nurse for God's sake. Shit! That sounds so sad... I'm a medical student at NIMS. There's something called doctors too, if you engineers care that is."

"Oh so you study at NIMS..."

"Ya... not sure about the studying part though." She chuckled. *Ah! She quoted me back to me.*

"And what about that day at the nursing home?" I dared to ask, hoping the conversation doesn't lead to the image of me lying helpless on a stretcher getting a shot.

"Oh there? I go there once every week... That nursing home is under NIMS... It's a part of our medical internship... That's all... And I'm not a nurse... Please!"

"Ya that's okay... I was mistaken..." I tried shifting the topic out of the nursing home premises.

"Hmmm... Okay then... it's quite late... 10.30 almost... I must leave..." she said taking out a wrist-watch from her cluttered bag and dropped it back. 'Why doesn't she wear it?' I wondered for a second.

"How will you go... It's far from here... more than four kilometers..." I asked.

"I'll have to find a conveyance"

"What conveyance?"

"I don't know... Let me see..."

"Let me see what? You won't get anything at this time... No buses... No cabs... No whatever..."

"Auto?"

"Ya... You might try for an auto... Though I doubt you'll get any..."

"Oh my god! Why engineers are so pessimist... Let me try at least..."

Engineers are pessimist because... Naah... Forget it... You've to be one to know that.

After around fifteen minutes of trying to stop speeding autos that went past us on the quiet night road, one of them stopped with sudden brakes, skidding the tires till a distance… *Burn rubber not soul.*

"NIMS Campus?" she moved forward and asked.

"NIMS… Hmm… One and a half on the meter-*awwwhhh…*" the driver said yawning.

He was drunk. I rightaway came to know. Cheap country-liquor reek filled my nostrils. He was a fat, dark and a hairy man… With prowl in his eyes and liquor in his paunch.

"Ok I'll go then… Nice meeting you Ali…" A slight curve adorned her lips and her right hand stretched out towards me for a handshake. *Pleasant.*

"Nice meeting you too… But I'll come along with you till NIMS." I said with a same courteous expression on my face. I could've successfully mocked her if it wasn't my ugly face.

"Why? I got an auto no… What happened?" she said looking at the waiting auto-*wala* who's paunch scratching and yawning had become almost violent by now.

"No… Nothing happened… Just let me come… I can be a bit too strange at times you know… Please." I persuaded.

"Ya… no probs with me… Only thing is how you'll come back to this place…"

"All that I'll manage… Now move into the auto… Fast." I interrupted and moved in after her, only hoping she would've understood the reason.

The auto *tuk-tuk*-ed to the NIMS Campus and we got down in front of the main building.

"So… why you came here?" was the first thing she said as the auto moved away.

"Hmm... The auto-*wala*... I didn't find him that good you know..."

"Good? Why are you supposed to find him good? Oh my god! What's up?" she broke into a guffaw... The sound of her laughter filling my ears.

"You forget it... This place is huge... Where you gonna go now?" I asked looking around, amused at her wit, her energy. *She loved her life.*

"There... You see there... Those windows... That's my hostel... And I can go there alone." She said pointing towards a distant building lost in the dense darkness. Only the windows were visible due to the lights inside.

"Ya sure you go alone... I don't even know how to get there." I said smiling at her.

"So bye at last... And you are a nice person Ali... Thanks again for what you did today." She said, this time not with a handshake.

"Bye..." I mumbled. An awkward silence followed, she turned and started walking.

My eyes didn't move until her image faded in the foggy dark night, she didn't look back.

National Institute of Mental Sciences was the biggest neurological sciences hospital in India. Doing a medical degree there meant that your school days were all about biology diagrams and microscopic slides. I had seen maniacs in student circles who, I know if given a chance, would happily give an arm to be in this college.

The vastness of the NIMS Campus testified the fact. Big banyan trees jutted out in abundance over the acres of land stretching out on both sides of Hosur Road, the buildings were old and classically constructed, back in the British rule. The lawns were wild, bushy and unkempt. The tree cover extended to roads at some places. And at this hour, it looked like I was stranded in a haunted forest.

"Where are you? Come to NIMS Campus and pick me up… Main gate… Fast!" I called Sandy whose cell was thankfully on now.

"I was about to sleep… I'm tired *yar*… Please" he said in a creaking voice.

"Come now… What tired? I'm alone here… Come fast!"

"Okay… I'll come. Wait at the main gate… And hey hold on… What the fuck are you doing at NIMS right now? It's almost 11."

"I didn't ask you the time. Come fast." I said cutting the call.

A collage of images and voices rushed through my mind… Image of the crowded BMTC bus, her bruised wrist, her yelling face, and then thankfully a smiling one. Voices of her hearty laugh, her *hey*s and her *oh-my-gods*, all repeated in my mind. I felt good for doing something good. I was feeling happy, not the hostel's surd Happy Singh… I mean I was feeling *happy*.

RX's sharp headlight pierced the fog and Sandy emerged.

"Here I am… Sit… Let's go."

I hopped onto the pillion. The RX pulled forward.

"Why were you there? That too at this time." He asked killing the engine as we reached the hostel gate.

"The bus dropped me there. It didn't come up till here…" I said.

"How? Which one you came by? See, 356B comes here directly … hmm… and 171 too. I don't think there's any bus which would come till NIMS but not cross BCE…" He started some bullshit. By the way I was the one throwing bullshit, no bus could ever abruptly stop at NIMS and not come to BCE, which was on the same straight road.

"Okay enough… Ask those BMTC people not me… And keep your cell on when you go out" I said as we reached the room.

I removed my Converse All-Stars and sank into the bed. Sandy offered the last before-bed Navy-Cut he was smoking, I somehow didn't like the smell.

I refused.

He was shocked.

I was thinking about her.

Sleep.

"Is Divya your friend? – Yes No"

My Orkut homepage flashed.

It had been three days since that meeting and just when I started having a doubt as to whether she had forgotten me, well, thank you Orkut.

I clicked yes and dropped her a 'hi'. I searched for her pic, there wasn't any, the display pic was shouting in big bold letters – '99% of doctors give the rest a bad name!' *Trying to be funny eh?*

Orkutting had gradually become boring and drab like throwing pebbles in a stagnant pond becomes after some time, but we still keep doing it. I too had grown sick and tired of monotonous hi's and sup's. Not to mention the legendary – 'Hi, I want to do frandship with you', which were ubiquitous in female profiles and the last four scraps in her scrapbook were on the same lines... *Frandship!*

"hi :)" I saw her scrap in my scrapbook. She was online. Orkut is great. Hail Orkut. Electrocute people who say a word against it.

"hi... you online??" I typed hurriedly.

"no... im not online... lol" was her prompt reply. *Got me!*

"ohk... so... ssup??" After the initial 'hi' stage was over, I knew nothing better to write on Orkut.

"nothing... getting bored in hostel..."

"me too" I replied, though she never asked me.

"u on gtalk??" she wrote after around five minutes. I thought she had gone offline. *Why Orkut can't clearly state who's online and who's not? But that's fine, Orkut's great.*

"ya... im..."

"then come on gtalk..." *Bye Orkut. I'm off to Gtalk. PS: You suck big time.*

Rightly so Einstein once said – "An hour sitting with a pretty girl on a park bench passes like a minute, but a minute sitting on a hot stove seems like an hour."

Though I had never tried the stove part, I knew it was true.

Our Gtalk conversation lasted for four hours straight, and as I saw the sun set outside the window, I was baffled at the speed of time.

When my dead dial-up connection suddenly became alive, we talked over the microphone.

And then when 'can't hear you!' happened, we talked with text.

Talk. Text. Talk. Text.

She was outspoken, smart and candid in her talk. Her parents stayed in Mumbai and she had a boyfriend there. The boyfriend turned out to be a two-timer and she showed him the middle-finger. She set her eyes on NIMS and made it look so easy. *Neat.*

We talked more, texted more.

She was friendly, responsive and knew how to keep a conversation alive, despite the gibberish I talked. She could playfully tease and banter and at the same time could sensibly talk matters of sex and puberty, unlike the prudes I had met till now.

She asked me to tell her about the guys' species found in BCE hostel, all uncensored, and when I did so, she replied with equal candor, equal bluntness.

I told her about male-breasted Kumar and how his assets would insecure even the *biggest* of females in college… she said it's got something to do with high estrogen levels.

I told her about feminine Mayank and how he fails to keep his ass steady at one place… she said it's got something to do with low testosterone levels.

I told her about ever-scratching Deepak and the difficulty he faces reaching his crotch when he wears a jeans… she said it's got something to do with an expired Itch Guard.

I told her about the increasing gay activities of the famous duo of Surender and Virender, and how I fail to understand how they go about it with each other… she said they'd know it better, why did it bother me? I was quiet.

And then I told her about Sandy and Raghu and the wild night-outs and marijuana sessions we have… she said it's got something to do with great friendships.

Talk. Text. Talk. Text. And then I signed out.

Four hours with her seemed like a minute. Had there been four continuous hours of Physics lecturer Iyer's class, I would have straightaway opted for death, no qualms about it.

I respected her frankness and openness, and within all that she had this aura of a composed yet poised girl who had set her goals, set her priorities, and set a definite limit for others.

I had become habitual of analyzing and grading girls based on their 'left right top and bottom'. But she was different from all I had met till now, all.

To be blunt, I somehow couldn't imagine her naked, or I didn't wanted to. Though over time and rigorous practice I had become a natural in the art.

I knew she kinda liked me for that day, though I also knew I was miles away of what she got as a first impression of me. I was an insensate and self-centered recluse with a loner mind... But I was not a faker, I was barefaced enough to say what I was as I was, maybe because I didn't care... *If that counts.*

One act of goodness, or one moment of following my impulse and I got to befriend someone whose first encounter with me was more befitting a response.

Her thoughts and her expressions revolved in my brain. I saved her number that she gave me and messaged her a 'good night'.

It was almost midnight and as I didn't get a reply, it was evident that she had slept.

I visualized her sleeping on her bed... innocence on her face, her black eyes partly closed, her long hair open, and maybe her mouth too.

I smiled.

Maybe she's crazy...

Days went by and the friendship between Divya and me, though remained only friendship, increased manifold.

Eventually NIMS became my second home as every other day we would go for long evening strolls in its tree-shaded environs. It was beautiful. I use to gripe about boring college life at BCE and she use to laugh at my stupid jokes... And within all the laughters and meaningless jokes, her company unknowingly started growing addictive to me... I loved her.

When not together, not more than an hour passed when we won't start messaging each other. We both knew it was more than just friendship, we both knew it was love, but it was more beautiful the unsaid way... I so loved her.

It was a clear Sunday morning just washed by rain. Sandy and I sat at the Sutta-point. Manju-bhai sat behind his counter reading the local newspaper, his USA shirt definitely needed a wash.

We missed the Sunday breakfast's *aloo parathas* which was the only good thing in the entire mess menu. Sandy had taken the responsibility of waking me up at 8 am, I was foolish enough to trust him and instead ended up waking him at 11 am.

I called out towards Manju-bhai for a chicken-rice. Sandy didn't order anything... the guy thinks he can survive on Navy-Cuts.

"Iyer... Iyer!!" Sandy shouted and in instant reflex I threw my cigarette away.

"Where? Fuck! Where is Iyer?" I asked him huskily, looking down at a newspaper kept on the table.

"Hey! What happened to you? I'm not talking about college's Iyer. Why will he come here? I'm talking about that Iyer." Sandy said pointing at the stray-dog who always hung around Sutta-point.

"What?? That dog? What the fuck *yar*?" I said repenting my cigarette.

"Ya... I named him Iyer... I know even a dog won't like that name but atleast then I can say things like 'Iyer licked my feet' or 'I fed Iyer with food scraps'... Ha!" he said looking contended towards the sky as if he just attained saintly enlightenment.

"Shove your shitty ideology up your ass! I had to throw my cigarette away..." I said and decided not to buy another.

My Navy-Cuts count had come down to just one a day, which was in the morning. I never had to try too hard to kick the habit, one night I didn't like the smell, next day I liked the smell but not too much of it too many times, and then came a stage when just one did the job. I could've easily kicked this too but deliberately didn't, just like that.

So now I never bought two Navy-Cuts and hence the second one didn't end with Raghu.

Of late Raghu had completely gone into hibernation, I seldom found him in the dorm-gallery and never visited his room in the seniors' wing.

His distance from me and Sandy, or any of his friends in that case, had increased. I knew Raghu was not the type who would study theoretical syllabus books whole day and won't move out of his room, nevertheless he would top. Maybe the year's gap that we shared was making a difference, whatever it was, I decided to leave him alone and shared small talk whenever I'd bump into him in the dinner mess. Neelam's face appeared in front of my eyes whenever I met him. I wanted to ask him one question – "How is she?" But better keep shut, I thought.

"wat u doin?" My cellphone beeped, it was her.

"nothin… chillin at sutta-point… missed d brkfast… u?" I replied.

"im havin a gala time :)" Came her answer.

"wat gala time? anythn special?" I asked.

"yup… my old boyfren frm mumbai is here… we're together again! i love him sooo much!" This was the moment I realised the kind of impact an SMS can have on you. It was like someone just pulled the rug from under my feet. *What is she saying? What does she mean? Is that so simple?*

"divya… wat r u sayin?" My trembling fingers replied.

"hey… aren't u happy? coming to see him?" Came her response.

"no… i guess i won't come… you ppl have fun… bye" And It's sometimes funny to see how fast a human brain can recover from a shock, or adapt to the reality that is.

A minute ago I was all blacked out and shattered, and now I wished her luck and simply wrote her 'have fun'.

"ali! u'll have to come… plsss… just come for a minute no… plsss :)" I couldn't ignore her, or my mind had become too inclined towards her trademark 'Plsss'-es. I decided to go.

"ya… i'll come. wait near the brown bench"

By now I knew every nook and corner of NIMS. We had our own set of meeting spots, the brown bench, the big clock, the paan-shop, the haunted tree. Our long walks from the Emergency Building to the OPD Building, from the Physiotherapy Block to the Rehabilitation Centre, these were the places where people came in hope of life. I too had found life here. *Life.*

Was I always just a friend to her? All those walks, all the time spent together, is the end to it so simple? Will I so simply get her out of my mind? Questions hounded in my head as I rode to NIMS.

I spotted her near the brown bench area and parked my bike and walked up to her. She was sitting on a Honda Dio scooter, her hair was disorderly and it looked like she was just coming from a ride. I tried hard to ignore her beauty, her innocent face her black eyes and the water in her eyes, her slender hands her delicate fingers and her unpainted nails. She looked so ugly… *I tried.*

"Hi" She said as I went and stood in front of her.

I just smiled.

"What happened to you?" She asked.

"Nothing."

"So… How did you like my boyfriend?"

"Where is he?" I asked looking around. The road was deserted as usual.

"What are you seeing around? See what I'm sitting on… My old scooty… It's back with me." She said trying hard not to laugh.

"Your scooty… What? This thing? Divya you were talking about this?" I said and let out a heavy sigh. My body loosened. I smiled. She was beautiful.

"Hah… Got you! And oh my god! Look at your face… You've turned white!" She said and finally burst out laughing. One of her typical laughs, spontaneous, hearty and full of life… *The best music I'd ever heard..*

"Whoooh… One word for you Divya… Crazy!" I said and pinched her nose.

"So you liked it?" she asked with a face reddened face and heavy breath.

"Liked what?"

"Liked the scooty you dumbo? You again want me to call it my boyfriend?"

"Ya it's good… And you kinda look funny riding it. So you got it ported from Mumbai?"

"No… Some guy rode it for 1200 kilometers."

"What???"

"Obviously I got it ported!"

Suddenly it struck me how dumbstruck I was, how my heart still raced at the thought of shaking hands with some guy who'll introduce himself as her boyfriend. Had it been some other female my only reaction would've been some swearing messages and a new hunt, but it was this crazy girl called Divya, who had driven me crazy too.

As Gnarls Barkley sang: *"But maybe I'm crazy… Maybe you're crazy… Maybe we're crazy… Possibly…"*

"So… Where you wanna go?" She asked.

"Oh, you're treating! That means you're really happy today huh..."

"Ya… Thought I'd treat you somewhere. Now tell fast… Where?"

"Hmmm… Anywhere… CCD again?" I said thinking the surroundings didn't matter until she was in it.

"Enough of CCDs and Baristas... I wanna eat something... How about Polynation?"

"As you say… Go park your scooty. I'll get my bike." I said taking out RX keys from my pocket.

"What? No… RX is out, Dio is in… I've had enough of your RX rides okay… Sit behind… Fast!"

Now it was my turn to laugh. She actually told me to sit behind her scooty. She rides while I sit on the pillion. And the funny part, she actually thinks I'll do so.

"Divya… What're you saying? Out of your mind eh? You think I'll sit behind you? Go park it fast…"

"What? Why can't you sit behind? I know how to ride you dumbo… Sit now."

"What why can't you sit behind? *Arrey,* ever seen a guy sitting on the pillion seat while the girl rides? That too I'm more than six feet tall okay... Are you nuts?"

"Ali! You male chauvinistic pig… You're gonna sit or not?"

Now there's a situation here. She calls me a pig. She calls me a male chauvinist. And then she expects this six feet tall guy to sit on the pillion-seat of a petty scooty that is being ridden by a girl. *Not a happening, at least in this birth.*

"You still thinking? Sit sit sit… Fast!" She exclaimed.

"Hey I told you *na*…"

"What told you? Try sitting once… Hey cut the crap and sit Ali…"

"But…"

"Plsss plsss plsss…"

It happened, this very birth, this very moment.

Looking downwards in embarrassment, I tried to fit myself in the rear seat of her new boyfriend. 'It isn't that uncomfortable by the way', I tried comforting myself.

"Hey take it easy… Remember I can just trip backwards okay!" I shrieked as she suddenly throttled the accelerator to the max and the scooty lugged forward.

We reached Polynation within an hour. She was a good rider, balancing it well in the heavy traffic, braking and honking at appropriate times, and her hard and fast rule - no talking while she rides. I constantly leaned forward to see the grave and frowned concentration on her face as she tactfully cut through the traffic... It was hard to believe.

Polynation was again one of those upscale restaurants in the Lifestyle Mall on Bangalore's MG Road. The lighting was dim and pale and even the afternoon was deliberately made to look like a cozy evening. Random strokes of paint brush, which was suppose to be perceived as great work of modern art, donned the walls. The seating arrangement was separate for fours and couples with ethnic jute and cane furniture spread all over. Most importantly it had maintained the trademark that its class of restaurants never let go – a complicated menu. Some strange surnames were attached to chickens and muttons, which was basically a desperate attempt at making them sound like continental.

Divya ordered some Chicken-Susan and Chicken-Cabbage-Blast... thankfully it didn't blast.

I didn't order anything as I wanted to eat what she ate, I liked the same taste to melt in my mouth as it did in her's. *Maybe I'm crazy...*

We soon walked out of Polynation, the afternoon was dull and our stomachs full. I pleaded with her to leave the scooty at the parking for now and we'd instead walk till the Brigades'.

Brigades' was one place in Bangalore where there was no question of one being unaware of it. From Auto-*walas* to any mortal who had spent a couple of days in the city, no one can escape this large and viscous cult of the Brigade Road. Though there was not much to talk of it, some best of restaurants in the city thanks to the complicated menu technique, best of showrooms which somehow survive on window shopping, a couple of huge book-shops that had made novel reading a fashion... and the best of couples that can be seen in Bangalore.

"I've some cash left... Let's go for Rock On... What say?" She broke the silence as we leisurely walked down towards INOX Multiplex at the Garuda Mall.

"Ya sure... But is it good?" I asked looking at the hoardings.

"It's amazing I heard... It stars Arjun Rampal you dumbo..." She said talking out her wallet. Even that was some ethnic jute stuff with beads and mirror-work. Why lately the whole of India was turning ethnic-chic?

"Arjun Rampal huh? Why should I be interested?"

The hoarding looked interesting. Four wild rebellious youngsters, long hair, lean bodies, aviator shades and fire-in-my-belly attitude. "Rock On!! – Live Your Dream." Screamed the title.

"You should be interested because you're gay!" she chuckled and pulled me by the sleeve towards the box-office.

We got the side-aisle seats somewhere in the middle row. The hall was as expected jam-packed. The movie begun, and so did a new chapter of my life.

Definitely not because of Arjun Rampal and not-so-Arjun Rampals in the movie, but I was liking it. Contemporary Indian Rock and the simultaneous progression of flashback and present was a new thing in Bollywood, and it clicked. More so the seating was cozy and comfy, the hall was dead dark, and she was by my side... Nothing more mattered.

'ye tumhari meri baatien... hamesha yoonhi chali rahen...' the song melted in our ears. She rested her head on my shoulder and snuggled up to me. Her hair smelt of her, her laughter, her eyes, her breath, better than a million Navy-Cuts, a million Marijuanas. I swept my hand over her hair and kissed her head, held her hand, her delicate fingers, got them close and kissed them.

We didn't talk a word. It was time eternity. Or I wanted the time to stop. I could've spent the rest my life in that position. Mellowing music, she resting on me, the fragrance of her hair, the crossing of our fingers. *I don't want heaven, just stop the fuckin time goddamnit.*

The pitch in the background picked and finally our lips met. I closed my eyes and images of all those meetings, those walks, the first time I saw her, all rushed through the darkness, and the warmness.

I clasped her fingers and didn't let my hands go where they could've gone. I somehow felt a guilt within me in touching her further. A guilt that she was so beautiful, a guilt that 'did I deserve her?', a guilt that 'what if I ever hurt her?'.

It was official, we were in love. Love which was no more a three letter word to me.

Though the world around me had changed within the three hours since I entered the theatre and moved out of it, it didn't seem that much of a change.

We walked till the Polynation parking where the scooty was parked. The night was clear and one of those unexpected Bangalore showers had just washed the roads, she kept to her chirpy and witty self and I preferred keeping shut on whatever that happened inside.

The only difference was now she clung on to my arm as we walked down the glittery Brigades', ruffled my hair whenever I cracked one of my numerous pathetic jokes and nudged me as I passed comments on some ultra-smooth pair of legs that turned this ordinary stretch of asphalt into what is Brigade Road today.

She didn't relent on my begging to let me ride the scooty. "Atleast till outside the parking Divya... What will that parking attendant think? What if he starts laughing? Fuck!" I pleaded literally folding my hands in front of her.

"Some other time preppy... Right now you sit behind..." She said with an air-kiss and for a moment I felt like a prep school going sissy girl.

"If that bastard laughs no..." I mumbled trying to fit my ass into the crammed area of the pillion seat.

"I seriously wish he does..." She said buckling her little helmet. The scooty moved forward, I jerked backwards.

He did control himself from laughing, but there was a smile on bastard's face.

"Stop here... I'll get down... My bikes parked there" I said removing the helmet from her head as we reached the brown-bench area of NIMS Campus.

It was almost 11 pm and the dry bushes surrounding the spot gave it a strange eeriness at night.

She braked and I at once jumped out of the backseat, or the self-embarrassment-seat.

I looked at her as she got down from her 'Chariot of Pride'.

"Hmmm... So tell me something... Why were you so pissed today when I told you that I got a boyfriend?" She asked getting her face inches away from mine.

"Umm... Eh... J-J-J-Just like that..." I said uncomfortably. I could hear her breathe.

"What is this J-J-J...? Now what happened to your tough guy status and all?" She said looking straight into my eyes.

"No actually..."

"Shut up!" She didn't let me finish, or even start.

"Okay..." I said trying to look anywhere but not into her deep dark black eyes.

"Do you mind?" She asked in the same whispering voice.

"Do you mind what?"

She moved forward and we lip-locked.

It was passionate. It was warm. It was magical. It was love.

I pulled her towards myself with my hands draped around her waist, but again, I didn't let them go where they could've gone.

'Why did you come here?' I remembered her asking me the first time we came to the same place around two months ago. I wanted to thank that auto-*wala*, for not getting a haircut and a shave, for drinking cheap Country-liquor that day, and then for drunken driving.

"I told you *na*... I got a special someone today." She said smiling... Sleep ready to takeover those eyes.

We talked like that for a while, her hands on my shoulders and mine around her waist. I know I was supposed to be the happiest guy on earth today, but I still didn't feel any major change whatsoever. I felt the same way for her as I felt yesterday, as I felt day before yesterday, or the day before that...

Kissing and cuddling hadn't suddenly shot-up my love for her, for it wasn't the same old get-in-get-out love anymore. I respected her trust in me and for a moment silently prayed to any Higher Power, if it existed, that I never break it.

I rode back to the hostel thinking about the day. Finally getting to ride my RX made me feel happy, not the hostel's Happy Singh though.

"Where were you?" Sandy asked as I entered the room.

"NIMS" I blurted by mistake.

"What? NIMS... Again at this time? Why now?" he asked aiming the butt of his last before-bed cigarette towards the trashcan... It didn't go in.

"Hmmm... What to do? Again the bus dropped me there..." I said picking the butt and dropping it in.

"Fuck you! I saw you came by bike asshole... You think I'm so dumb?"

"Ya whatever... Umm... Let's talk about this in morning..." I desperately tried to escape.

"My ass." he said and disappeared into his large blanket. And as usual the pajamas and t-shirt he wore came out from the side. Even in chilling Bangalore cold, Sandy liked to sleep naked... Thankfully with his boxers on. Thankfully stripping under the blanket.

I picked up my cellphone to message her 'good night', the Inbox still had the message – 'ya... my old boyfren frm mumbai is here... we're together again! i love him so much!'.

I played *'ye tumhari meri baatien...'* and sunk into my bed.

The song surrounded me by her feel and thus bounded me to smile.

Sleep.

> Black-skinned, stone-eyed, sharp-toothed.

"Hi" I said as I went and sat next to Raghu in the dinner mess. The dinner time was almost over and the mess was empty by now. I was as usual late because of a place called NIMS, and he because of an obsession called solitude.

"What's up Ali… Why late?" he said with a smile. His smile had become somewhat formal now, a restrained one. I wished he would've been downright snobbish, atleast I won't feel like getting faked then.

"I'm fine *yar*… What's up with you?" I said ignoring the 'late' part.

"I'm doing good too… How's Sandy?"

"Sandy's fine… Why don't you come to the room now *yar*? Atleast for a couple of smokes…" I said looking at him.

He kept quiet. I knew I had asked something stupid… But I didn't know why it was stupid.

"How are studies going on?" I asked the same old lame question, trying to shift the topic.

"Studies are going good… Your's?" He replied. I smiled within at the kind of conversation we were having. *How are your studies going? Shit!*

"Fine fine… They're fine…" I said and stuffed in the cold curry rice somehow.

A silence prevailed. Only the sound of our munching mouths oscillated. I decided to keep shut and leave it that way.

"Listen Ali… You're my friend and I wish I could answer all your questions okay… but that's not gonna help you or take you anywhere…" Raghu suddenly spoke looking at me. The spoon from his hand dropped into the rice.

"Hmm… See Raghu… I don't know what's gotten over you… But I know you're not a fool like us and you'll face it and show that to the world… You'll fuckin show that to the world… And I'm by your side… Always." I said keeping a hand on his shoulder as if consoling him. Raghu never needed any consolation whatsoever. A fool consoling him is actually consoling himself.

"Thanks *yar*… And It's fine… Not that much of a big deal…" he said returning to the meal.

Again a silence prevailed. Our mouths munching. I decided to break it this time.

"How's Priya? Is anything wrong with her?" I asked trying to make it as casual as possible… I knew it wasn't.

"What? Priya? Now you care about Priya?" He said looking straight towards me. His tone direct and clear. I tried to shift my gaze.

"No what I mean is…"

"Shut the fuck up Ali!" he said almost raising his voice. "Why you want to show you're bothered when you aren't? That way you can't get away with me okay… You say hi, I say hi, and then it might lead to a 'how are you?'… But then comes a line… Keep off it…" he said wiping off the last specks of rice from his plate.

I kept quiet. Anything I speak now can turn against me. Though I too had finished my meal, I decided to get up a minute after Raghu, that way I won't have to walk alongside him.

Raghu returned and again sat next to me, this time looking calm, his hand on my shoulder, "See Ali… I don't want to be that asshole who shouts at his friends when angry and then returns to them with a high-five when times are good… I just prefer to keep my mouth shut when there's a rough patch."

"Hmmm…" I said, hoping that won't cause any damage.

"You might even care for Priya… By the way you always call her Neelam… No big deal I'm just telling you. But why ask something when you can't do any shit about it... I mean what in the world can we do to get her out of there? And when you casually ask me how is she doing and all, should I say she's doing good? A girl who lost her virginity before her puberty is doing good? I know I'm insane to think about her and that's what I'm trying… Trying to get her out of my mind… Out of my fuckin mind… And again… I can't do shit about it."

"I understand…" I said after he kept silent for a while.

"Ya… I hope you understand… Because you too have a dark side… You too have a nostalgia that haunts you from the past… And you too can't do shit about it… You're just too happy ignoring it and looking the other side…"

His last words sent a chill down my spine. Goosebumps ran through me and I asked frustrated, "What dark side and all you talking about? What nostalgia? I'm fine… Very fine…"

"You might have forgotten what you told me but I haven't… About that old friend of your's… Hmmm… What was his name…" He said trying hard to recall.

"Gopal" I interrupted.

"Ya Gopal… You can't get him out of your mind and you don't know why… This is what happens Ali… I'm not wishing anything bad for you… I hope you get to bump into him sometime in your life and again you both play together like old pals… But all that's just wishful thinking… Reality is that it forms a chunk in your brain and you just can't get over it… A fucking chunk… I kept shut when you opened up about Gopal and let it all come out... But now when I'm trying to get something out of my mind... And you can't do anything about it... Then why not just shut that pie-hole."

He laughed as he said the last line. The laugh was strange but it was not faked. It was a laugh that can make one suddenly realise the dumb expression on his face, and in this case it was me.

I washed my hands and deliberately waited until Raghu moved out of the mess gate. His words were too harsh and too direct, but they were true. *They were true.*

I walked into the room and '*Zehreelay*' from 'Rock On!!' played on Sandy's 15000 watt woofers. He lay on the floor hysterically doing push-ups... I know seeing the 'sonofabitch' guy in Café Mocha that day had taken a toll over him.

"Wear something..." I shouted towards his boxer clad up-down oscillating body but it got lost in the earsplitting beats of '*Zehreelay*'.

'Rock On!!' had managed to pull some real western sounding hard-rock numbers. '*Zehreelay*' topped the list. It had everything what rock should have... Frenzied screaming and screeching, smelting guitar-solo and most importantly a hidden meaning in the lyrics.

The vocalist sings in fiery rage – 'This world is full of venomous snakes... Black-skinned, stone-eyed, sharp-toothed, venomous snakes... They silently wait for an opportunity to sting you... And sooner or later, they will sting you... You can run but not for long... Ultimately, they WILL sting you..."

The meaning of these snakes is left upto the listener. It can be anything, a lover's broken heart, a teenager's peer-pressure, an addict's heroin habit, a nostalgic memory from the past... Anything. And you can't run away from thinking about it... The snake will sooner or later bite you for sure.

Everyone has these snakes, whether he's aware or not. For me they were unending thoughts and memories of Gopal. Venomous snakes from the past that had successfully crept their way into my head. The children's park, the mall, the cycling club… All disguises of those snakes. *Big black merciless snakes.*

Why did Raghu remind me of Gopal today? Why when life seems so utopian something comes and vandalizes it all? I looked at a box of Navy-Cuts lying on Sandy's bed. I wanted a puff. One deep dark puff.

"You know you're gonna flunk out if you keep visiting me like this…" Divya said with a chuckle.

It was almost 7 pm and the sun was calling it a day. The sky was reddish-orange loaded with black clouds. The brown-bench area was as usual dark and looked like an ideal set for a low-budget horror movie… Though I had managed to shoot a love story there.

"Hmmm… Ya you are right… I might flunk … So now all contacts cut for a month… I'll just study okay…" I said trying to get grimness on my face.

"Hey nooo… I was kidding. You're saying you won't come for a month… Are you nuts?" She said suddenly blocking the way.

"Then… Why are you acting smart?" I said with extreme pride of getting to fool her for the first time.

"Oh that was very funny… You know *na* that you're one dumb-ass." She said as we again started walking.

"Hmmm… No… I don't keep misconceptions."

"No you're dumb… I can prove that you are… Save yourself by

proving you aren't…" She said punching her fist on my back. It was hard but I didn't let it come on my face. *Fuck! She's strong.*

"And how will you prove that?" I said trying to smile.

"See… A cute smart and good looking girl like me won't go out on a coffee with you…" She said with an air of a Miss World.

"What is that self-praise by the way?" I asked.

"Oh whatever… Let's just say… A cute smart and good looking girl won't go out on a coffee with you." She said and now I had to give a calculated answer which would decide my DQ – Dumb Quotient, an acronym just made up in the of NIMS Brown-Bench area.

"Hmmm… Well I won't ask her out in the first place." I decided to remain on the safer side. Other witty answers for sometime else, when my DQ is not at stake.

"Well that's what makes you dumb." She said and burst out laughing.

"Umm… Ah… I..." I had lost it. It was over.

She was laughing and if that makes her laugh, then I'd want to be a million times dumber. A DQ so low that she laughs forever and never gets a frown on her face. I bent and kissed her cheek. We kept walking the same way, hand in hand, time eternity.

"Hey mess will close… 8.20… I'll have to go…" She said looking at my watch.

"It's only 8.20… Go later… Mess won't close so early." I said somehow trying to stop her till nine. If she goes before nine, then I'll have to wait for her to come back. That is how it was formulated between us - no one goes back before nine.

"Mess now closes at 8.30… So if you're trying to make me stop till nine… I don't know… We'll eat outside and you pay…"

"What? Eat outside? No no… You go I'll wait here…" I said knowing the fact that she can suddenly become serious on the 'eat outside' part, and considering the numerous expensive treats that she had spent on me, I was in a serious position to return.

"Then wait here... I'll come in...hmmm... 10 minutes..." She said and slid her hand from mine.

"Come soon..." I said smiling at her. The usual 'wait for me' time begun.

Her '10 minutes' were never ten minutes, they could be 20, 30 and even 40 if she liked the food... And given the fabulous mess food at NIMS Hostel, anyone would. The dishes which were a distant memory for us were a daily for them, all at government subsidized fees.

I had my own ways of spending these '10 minutes'. Catch up with an old friend on phone, recall and calculate the week's expenses, think of some clever lines to speak when she comes back, or just sit idly and look at the vastness of NIMS Campus.

I remembered noticing some clutch and gear problem in the RX while riding to NIMS and decided to check it in the meantime by taking a ride in the campus.

The bike started and the same striking sound erupted in the engine as it moved forward. In front of me was a dark narrow road where visibility was impossible had it not been the dim headlamp of the RX. I didn't stop or turn the bike and it led me into the road. *Or destiny led me into that dark alley.*

I changed gears and repeatedly kept looking down at the gear-box, unknown of the fact where the slow moving bike was taking me. *Or where the destiny was taking me.*

I suddenly stopped the bike noticing I had come very deep into the bushy campus. There was darkness so thick that I couldn't see the bike I was sitting on when the headlamp switched off.

But for a moment that it switched off, I noticed a dim light by the roadside just steps away from me. The light was coming from basement window of a small two-story building. I directed the headlamp towards the building, it was old and weary, flakes of yellow paint hung from its withered walls. But I could feel there was life inside it, someone told me from within to get down the bike and see behind the iron mesh of the basement window. *'Get down and go do it Ali. Get down and do it'*

I slid down the side-stand and got off the bike. Pieces of dry-grass crumbled under my feet as I walked towards the pale-yellow light of the window. I bent down to the max to get a view through the thick and dusty iron-mesh. *I wish it was thicker. I wish it was dustier. I wish I wouldn't have been able to see inside.*

A dim electric bulb provided the only source of light in the small room. A few men in soiled white clothes lay on the floor, some of them sleeping, some leaning against the wall, but all of them there from long. My eyes stopped at one face whose drowsy eyes were expressionlessly fixed at the slow ceiling-fan.

I've seen him somewhere. I know the face. Blood rushed into my head. My body became rock solid as if big python snakes suddenly wrapped themselves around me. *Big black merciless snakes.*

I know that fucking face goddamnit.

I want to break the mesh and jump inside, at the same time I want to run away, run until I see this earth as a small marble. I want to lift my hands and wipe my sweat but they're fixed due to the snakes. I want to get rid of them but they won't get off… They are here and they are strong and they won't get off.

I know the fucking face goddamnit. The face is Gopal.

What the fuck is happening? He is Gopal.

Marijuana or Vodka…? Or reality?

And just like that, destiny got me into some deep dark narrow road, destiny made me peep inside an old building in a Government Mental Hospital… And destiny took me to Gopal. *You can run but not for long, ultimately they WILL sting you.*

The ringtone of my cellphone suddenly pierced through the darkness, I stumbled to hold it steady and tried to read the flashing name. It was her. I looked around and some reality started to sink in.

The ride which I had started to check that gear and clutch problem in my RX had taken me to Gopal, I was squatting to an old building deep into the NIMS Campus and Gopal lay in front of me. I cut the call and again collected the guts to look inside, the lights were off, they were off now and even the iron-mesh couldn't be seen, only the light of my cellphone cut through the thick darkness.

It again rang, again the sound pierced through the darkness and my ears alike. I stumbled and pressed the cut button, I thumbed it long and hard and the phone switched off.

I hurriedly crawled back and got up and ran towards the bike. I wished running away from what I saw was also that easy.

I try to grip the RX key from the ring but it seems the most difficult job in the world. I try to insert it in the panel but now this seems the most difficult job in the world. I kick down and try to ignite the bike but nothing before seemed more difficult. Eventually the bike moves forward but keeping it balanced makes landing an air-plane look easy.

I straight away head towards the main road and eventually to the hostel, barring all red-lights and never letting the speedo go below 80.

At last I found my room, my bed, my four-walls. There are no iron-meshs here neither there is any darkness. But there are snakes, not in the room but within my veins. *Big black merciless snakes.*

"Where were you *yar*? And what's this fucked up expression on your face?" Sandy asked looking up from his push-ups position.

"Nothing..." I tried to talk more and come into reality forgetting whatever just happened. But whatever just happened was the real reality.

I jumped into my bed and tried to feel an ending of just another day. Tried to feel like I had just returned from one of those evening strolls with Divya, and tried to think of whatever we talked today, like everyday. But all I could think of was one image, one face... A tiredly rotating fan, a small dark room, and one face.

I switched on the cellphone and saw the time, 10.00 PM, beeps of missed call alerts and messages rang one after another. 16 messages, all of them her's, all asking 'whr r u?' 'wht hppnd?' 'im waitin near the bench' '???'. I wished I could simply reply the usual one 'my phone was off by mistake' or 'i ws sleeping my heads off'.

But what am I suppose to say now? 'hey u kno i jus saw my old slum fren in some building in ur campus... eeks... he looked so weird...' or 'hey u kno this worlds such a small place... i jus saw my fren whom i had last seen yrs ago in delhi... cool no?'

This is it Ali. You've seen Gopal today. What is he doing here? How did he come here? What is that building? What is that room? You don't know anything. The snakes are staring at you in the face... And you can't do shit about it.

The cellphone rung again, that same ringtone, for a moment it took me back to that darkness. I shook my head and came to terms with present, her name flashed on the screen.

I pressed the green.

"Hey Ali… Where were you from so long? Why were you not picking? You told you'll wait right?" She would have asked a thousand more questions had she not sensed my rapid breathing.

I kept quiet. Her voice was beautiful.

"Ali? Are you there? Talk to me... What happened?"

"Oh… N-Nothing… Nothing happened… What were you saying?" I said letting out heavy sighs.

"Where did you go? I was waiting… Your cell was also off. Is everything okay Ali… Why are you breathing so hard?" She asked. I tried to visualize her worried face asking all those questions. But only one face flashed. *One goddamn face.*

"I'm okay… Just a bit tired… I think I'll sleep…" I said trying to control my breathing.

"But why did you disappear suddenly … You know I got worried. And now you're simply saying you'll catch some sleep. You didn't even bother to drop a message. You're such an uncaring jackass Ali…" Her words were choking and I know she wanted to cry. She wanted to cry because I didn't care for her.

I too wanted to cry. Wanted to cry to lose some weight off my head. To taste my tears like a pacifier. But no. Crying was something that was long gone from my anatomy. There were times I felt sad. Felt extremely sad. Felt extremely victorious and jumped in screams of jubilation. And then helplessly watched the motions of defeat. All those times, my heart cried. It cried and it cried loud and bad. But my eyes never cried. I tried but they didn't. My heart told them to but they didn't.

"No… No listen… I do care for you Divya… I'm sorry… It's just something rather strange that happened to me… That's all… I… I love you and care for you… Please don't cry…" I said tightly shutting my eyes and opening them again wishing everything would return to normal.

"Ya… Enough of your drama… Now tell me what happened… I know all strange things end up happening with you… And you're a certified dumbo today…" She said laughing.

"It's not funny Divya…"

"Ya… I'm serious… That is proved… You're dumb and there's nothing funny about it… Oh my god, why am I laughing…"

"It's not funny… I've never forgotten to message you or call you… But I'm sorry today I didn't. You'll never understand what happened today… And even if you do, you'll not understand what it means to me. Sorry again for making you sad. Let's talk later. Good night." I said and cut the call without even waiting for her to speak. Cut.

I lay on the bed staring at the mosquitoes buzzing on the ceiling when the phone rang again. Again that ringtone.

"Hey sorry sorry sorry… I'm serious now… Tell me what is it…" She said from the other end.

"Divya… Chill… It's not that big… And it makes no difference to you… Talk about something else if you want to." I said trying hard to stop myself from shouting 'shut the fuck up!'.

"No tell me about it… You told I won't understand. What makes you think that? Tell me or I'll keep bugging you…"

I took a deep breath and got up in sitting position. I knew I'll need her help in knowing about that building, that road, those men, and I'll have to tell her the truth.

"Listen. There is a road leading inwards from the brown-bench area. A dark and bushy road. You wouldn't have seen that so I don't know how to tell you the exact location... Hmmm..."

"I know that road... Carry on." She broke in.

"You know the road?"

"I think I study here... Carry on." She said bluntly.

"Oh ya right... So by mistake today I went to that road and saw a building. An old yellowed building... It was two-storey tall and..."

"I know the building... What happened next?" She again pitched in.

"Ok good... So what happened next eh? What happened next was that..." I suddenly stopped. What actually happened next suddenly flashed in front of my eyes. *How do I tell her 'what happened next'? Is it as simple as 'what happened next'?*

"Ali... Speak!" She shouted in the microphone.

"What happened next is something you won't understand Divya. You'll just find it stupid." I said again trying to get off the image from my mind.

"Still you tell me... Fast... Tell... I'll understand..."

"I went and peeped inside the basement of the building. There I saw..." I stopped.

"What? I'm waiting... Just say what you saw Ali... Then I'll tell you something... Fast... Just say what you saw." She interrupted into my silence.

"Hmmm... What I saw eh? I saw an old friend of mine lying there on the floor in a totally fucked up condition..." I said in a single breath and waited for her response. I was frustrated. I wanted this to end... *End the melodrama and let me sleep goddamnit.*

"Friend as in? What friend you saw there? What fucked up condition?" She asked in a voice so plain that it made clear all this was just a story to her.

"Friend as in my old friend whom I had not met for the last six years. He was the only friend I had in my childhood days... And... And somehow his thoughts and memories always haunted me Divya... Hmmm... And... And that's all... Enough." I said closing my eyes and trying to stay calm. No part of it I wanted to recall more. I just saw a friend, that's it.

"See. First of all... That building is the old NIMS Mental Asylum block. Inmates have now been shifted to a new bigger block. So you seeing your old lost friend and all there means you were high or something... Marijuana? Or maybe Vodka? What did you had Ali?" She said laughing. Her laugh was sarcastic and sent a frenzied fit of anger down me.

"I wasn't high Divya... I don't drink. I said you'd not understand." I said trying to keep my cool. *Breathe deep. Keep your cool. It's not her fault.*

"No... You were... Or maybe you'd have fallen asleep and had one of your stupid dreams... You took so long to tell me such a stupid thing you dumbo... By the way nice imagination... Good job..." She said and laughed me off. A chuckle, a laugh, a giggle... and that was all it meant to her.

Keep your cool. Keep your cool. Keep your cool. NO!

"Listen you bitch! I'm trying to tell you something that shattered the world around me and you find reasons to laugh in that... What part of this is funny to you? WHAT PART? See Divya... Life's not always rainbows and butterflies okay... And if it is for you then shut the fuck up and leave me alone... You getting me? LEAVE ME FUCKIN ALONE!!" I said and threw the phone away. The frenzied anger had shown its form. The phone went and hit the wall, so did my relationship with her.

I know I had shouted, and I had shouted bad, but seeing Sandy get up from his sleep and stare at me… I realised the real intensity of my shout. Last time I had to play Himesh Reshamiya on his 15000 watt woofers to wake him with that expression on his face.

"What's up with you? Who you shouting at? Who was it?" he asked still staring blankly.

"Nobody… You go back to sleep." I said looking down.

"Who's Divya?" he asked. I raised my head in shock. He was standing right next to me. Only boxers.

"How do you know her?" I asked taken aback.

"Your phone… Last received. Take it..." He said handing me the mobile. It was working but had a broken screen. My anger didn't prove that expensive.

"Oh… You saw in the phone…" I said relieved.

"And heard you shouting also… Who's she… You were calling her bitch…" He said going back to bed.

"What!!! I called her bitch??? I what??? Are you sure?" I asked getting up in response.

Such was the spell my mind was in. The anger was mixed with depression and I had no control or memory of what was coming out.

"Listen you bitch! This is how you started. And it was loud man… Loud…" He said shaking his head and smiling in amusement.

"Fuck! What do I do now? I thought I'll talk to her tomorrow but now… What to do? Oh shit… Shit shit shit!" I dropped down on my knees and squeezed my face in regret.

"Hey… Hey… Ali you okay… Who's the girl yar?? You're on your knees… Whoa!" He said waving at me.

"Fuck you! Get into your blanket or I'll kill you! You're the bitch not her!" I shouted and the irritating smile on his face suddenly disappeared. He too.

What do I do now? I called her bitch. Can someone rewind my life's cassette? Just once. Just five minutes.

I tried to call her but her cell was off. On the broken screen of my cell, I tried to read what I typed.

"divya... listen... im sorry 4 whtevr i shouted... i went out of my mind. dunno how to apologise... jus rembr i luv u n nvr wana hurt u... pls dont cry... abuse me bt pls dont cry."

Message Sent.

I dropped into my bed and stared at the ceiling. I wanted to cry, again my heart was crying but my eyes weren't. I wanted to cry and taste my tears, but the eyes didn't listen... *They just don't listen.*

The night was deep and cold wind whistled outside. The image of that road, the building, the fixed eyes, all flashed on-off in front of me.

I knew Divya was crying and I wanted to wipe her tears and hug her into myself.

Wanted to tell her that she is not a bitch. Infact Sandy is. Or anyone is but not her.

I want to make her laugh by acting dumb. Want to sit behind the scooty and curse the parking attendant. Want to crack stupid jokes and feel the ruffle in my hair.

I stared at the ceiling aimlessly.

The day was long, but again, finally it was over... Or I hope it was.

Any Higher Power, if you exist, give me the strength...and some sleep.

Sleep.

"I thought you quit smoking." Manju-bhai said as I reached his counter for another pack of Navy-Cuts.

Two days since I saw Gopal. Two days since I went to college. Two days since bath and hairbrush. Two days since two packs everyday.

Her phone never switched on. My Outbox had 20 messages, Inbox had none.

"Hmmm... *Maachis?"* I asked ignoring his expression.

"What's the matter?" he said reaching out with his lighter.

"Thanks." I said and turned around to sit outside Sutta-point.

"What's the matter Ali? Come here and tell me. Don't go. Come here and tell me." His words were straight and when Manju-bhai speaks in that tone, one can't insult him and brush him off. That'd mean losing a friend, and the credit account facility at Sutta-point.

"Tell you what Manju-bhai?" I asked reaching his counter.

"Tell me why are you not attending classes? Then this heavy smoking? You know what you've to tell me..."

"I'm in a bit of depression Manju-bhai. I'll hopefully get over it soon. Just a phase..." I said as smoke rolled out of my nostrils.

"Hmmm... Just a phase eh? It's ok if you don't wanna tell me. But I tell you what Ali... Remember that at your age every second thing seems like depression and the end of the world. Either you fuck yourself by smoking your heads-off which will eventually lead to all kinds of drugs and shit. Or have the courage to face the real world. Trying to escape the reality by going high and all is gonna lead you to a point of no return... And kids like you have no idea how bad that point of no return can be... How bad."

"I'm not a kid anymore Manju-bhai..." I murmured trying to smile at him.

"Then stop acting like one. You're doing what kids do. Ever seen them playing hide and seek? You're trying to play hide and seek with your problems..."

I laughed at the thought of hide and seek. *Hah! Hide and seek.*

"May sound like too much of gyaan to you, but I'm telling you all this now because I know you're a good guy at heart Ali. And you know I'm right... Just think of your problem... Don't tell me just think of it... Whatever it is... Just think of it..."

He was silent. The images that I was trying to forget again became clear. All the fade on the pictures flew off and that night became alive again.

"Isn't there a better way of solving it than these sticks you're sucking? Tell me isn't there any...?"

I nodded. Obviously there was a way. Cut the emotional drama. Go to NIMS. Get him out of there. Period.

"Yes there is a way Manju-bhai..." I tried to stiffen my body and dared to speak the truth.

"If you know there is a solution to your problems then go get it Ali... Just go get it... It hurts me to see you like this... Any help you need and I'm there... Any help..."

I'll never forget that conversation with Manju-bhai. Sitting there on the Sutta-point bench, I dared to think of what had happened with me straight and clear. I realised that calling Divya bitch, or even Sandy, was not gonna help. I'd turn out to be that same asshole who shouts at his friends when angry, and returns to them with a high-five when times are good.

I stared at the burning Navy-Cut and realised it's the cigarette that does the smoking, the person just sucks. *Just sucks.*

I'll get back to Divya and make her laugh again. I'll get to the root of it and get Gopal out of there.

But I didn't know the ups and downs that awaited me. And that the lows of real world are far stronger than the highs of a million drugs. *A million of them.*

"And don't say this to everyone okay... Otherwise I'll lose all my cigarette sales..." Manju-bhai called out towards me with a hearty, healthy laugh. I wished I too could laugh like him. Till two days ago I had.

"i dun think u're even readin my msgs... but if u're... then lemme tel u tht i promise 2 say sorry n mak u laugh agn... if not today then tmrw... n im not on any marijuana or vodka... i jus need u n u're my high... my world... bye n tc. certified dumbo"

Message Sent.

Hail the Puppet Master

The evening was overcast and I sat staring at the four walls of my room. I thought about all that Manju-bhai had said in the morning.

The same old troublesome voice was echoing in my head – *'Be a man and stand up on your legs Ali'* it said... and I stood up on my legs. Literally.

I got up hard and strong. Put on my shoes and wind cheater and set out in the cold evening.

7.20, I saw the time on cellphone's broken screen as I sat on my RX in front of the hostel.

With an ultimate decisive sigh, I decided to fire it and go to NIMS.

The emptiness around the brown-bench area looked more haunting without her. Dark and gloomy bushes, moths making that continuous droning sound, and dry grass crunching under my shoes as I stood in front of that road. Everything was reminding me of her, and I was busy ignoring all of it trying to collect the guts to ride to that road again.

"...there is a new Mental Asylum block..." her words resounded into my head. Going into the same dark alley had become impossible for me now, I found my hands shivering and my forehead sweating profusely despite the cold.

I read the Campus Map display board and straightaway head to the new block.

The huge Asylum building stood in front of me as I parked the RX and walked inside.

I had my actions clear in my mind. Talk to the doctor there. Get to know why and how he's here. And then think about getting him out.

I was directed to the visitor's room. The galleries, the white dress people, the stretchers, the wheel-chairs, all of them had that same eerie creepiness. That same silent cry which echoes in every single hospital ever existed...

I waited in the huge waiting room, the evening was giving way for night and the silence around me was further discomforting.

I looked around the hall, an old woman sat in the other corner with a young head-shaven boy whose face wore a numb expression. A sweeper was cleaning the floor and spreading the creepy smell of disinfectants which got mixed with the emptiness of the hospital air and sent jitters down me.

"Wait for the night shift doctor... He'll come in half-an-hour..." A man appeared in front of me and said with an expressionless face. Before I could reply or say anything, he turned around on his toes and walked away.

8 pm, I saw the time and moved out of the building to get rid of the air inside.

I sat on my parked RX and lighted a Navy-Cut.

I thought of her. Her dark eyes her deep voice and the feel of her cold palms on my cheeks.

I thought of Gopal. How I had met him again in my life. How he must've spent his days there.

A sudden beep in my cell cut through the silence around.

It was her.

"hi... hw r u?? wat u doin??" the screen flashed.

So here it was. Her response. After my 36 messages and infinite missed calls, here it was. *"hi... hw r u?? wat u doin??"*

"im fine... talk 2u l8r... right now im sitting in front of the new asylum block... waitin fr the doc... n sorry agn." I replied.

Now there are defining moments in everyone's life, whether they're aware or not. I too had one of them, when all of a sudden my cell again beeped with her message.

"y u alws wear this white shirt... makes u look so dumb..."

I read and suddenly raised my head from the screen.

And there she was... Walking towards me with her smile adorned face.

Seeing her in that precise moment, I realised how vulnerable I had become in the last two days. How badly my eyes longed to see her... How I ever lived without her.

"Come..." she said pulling me by the wrist.

"Come? Come where Divya? Wait... I... I've to talk to the night-shift doctor here..." I said taken aback by her first reaction.

"What doctor? What do you think you're doing Ali? Get off the bike and come with me... I've to tell you something... Otherwise why do you think I've come all the way in this night-suit itself?" She said staring at me. I looked at her and smiled. Same black eyes, same innocent face, same hair strands falling on to it.

"What you smiling at?? Come!!"

What am I smiling at? Even I'll never know that... And I don't wanna either.

I silently got down and we walked till the rear side of the building.

The place was dark and empty and I almost instantly asked, "What is it Divya? Tell me now..."

"Ali. Just answer me okay... What did you see that day in the old Asylum building?" she said looking straight into my eyes.

I spoke after a pause, "See Divya… Let's not talk about all that. It has already caused so much trouble…"

"What did I tell you? Just answer me." She said interrupting me.

"Hmmm… It just happened that I saw inside that building. There were a few men inside and I knew one of them. I know you think I was high or whatever… But I know what I saw. Best would be that we don't talk about this…" I said looking at my watch. 'It's 8.30, the doctor would've come' I thought.

"And what are you doing here in this building at this time?" she asked.

"I came to talk about that thing. The night-shift doctor would've come by now… You just wait outside… I'll come…" I said pulling her to walk back towards the front-side.

"Ali. Wait. Wait here and listen to me. I'm sorry for that day. You were right. There are people in that building. Whatever you said was right… They're in a pretty fucked up condition. I went with my friend to check and we were caught by the security guard there… He has shut even that one window now. And I already did what you're going to do today… I asked the doctor about it, but he is not replying. He says that there is no one in that building and all inmates are shifted to new premises… But you know what the truth is Ali? The inmates in that building are unaccounted in NIMS record… Their identity could not be known and they're just rotting there… No one knows about them and even their records are non-existent… You listening to me Ali…"

She suddenly shook me up seeing my expressionless face.

What is she saying? Unaccounted means what?

"What're you saying Divya… Unaccounted means what? Is there any procedure to get them out now?" I asked feeling my head was throb as I tried to sync her words.

"Unaccounted means that their identity is unknown to NIMS... So they just put them in that building. Getting them out is impossible Ali... The doctors are not ready even to talk about them... I'm a student so I asked some teachers and seniors and all... There is a security-guard at that building and now you can't even go close to it now... NIMS is India's biggest mental hospital and all these cases are common here. We can't do anything about it Ali..." She said shaking her head.

Her last words hit me hard – We can't do anything about it Ali – *You can't do shit about it Ali.*

"But... Still let me talk to the doctor once..." I said trying to console myself.

"Talk to the doctor? This is a government hospital Ali... If he gets pissed then he can just call the police and get you in for case of trespassing into that area... It's not as simple as it looks... Talking to the doctor will finish even the slightest ray of hope..."

Ray of hope? She thinks there is?

"What ray of hope? What's that slightest ray of hope you just said...?"

"Hmmm... After all this... Still if you're really serious about it... Then you can use some contacts or something..."

"What contacts?" I interrupted.

"Relax Ali... NIMS is a government hospital after all... If you know someone here... Or maybe say bribe someone here... You can sneak him out... But that is just my thinking..."

"Bribe whom? That security guard?"

"See... All that I don't know... I just thought of it and told you..." she said.

I nodded and kept quiet.

"And I got all your messages..." She said and rested her arms around my shoulders.

Suddenly all the throbbing in my head and the bruises it suffered in last two days came to a rest. She was with me at last. Her flawless face reflecting in the moonlight and those black watery eyes fixed on me... The world can wait.

"You did so much for me... Sorry for what I said..." I broke the silence.

"Ya... You called me bitch no? How dare you..." She said laughing and punched me hard on my stomach. I tried smiling but couldn't even come close to it.

"A-a-a-i-i-i said sorry no... How do you hit so hard Divya? You don't even seem so strong..." I said with my eyes out of their sockets.

"But I'm strong... And I hit you because I can smell you just smoked..." she said and pulled me ahead.

"Oh my god... Your punches would kill me before those cigarettes can..."

We walked and talked for a while, and for that while, life again seemed utopian and all the voices in my head drowned out to her laughters and giggles.

I then rode to the hostel thinking about her one message that stopped me from meeting the doctor and hence meeting more trouble.

The smell of her hair, her night-suit, her breath, still lingered around me... And the grinding in my stomach reminded me of the punch.

Just as the bike approached BCE campus and I thought another long day would come to an end. It' didn't.

The lights inside Manju-bhai's house, above Sutta-point, were still on.

'...any help you need and I'm there. Any help...' I thought of Manju-bhai's words and turned the bike towards Sutta-point.

10.40, I saw the time as I stood in front of the door. I finally decided to knock.

"What?? You want someone out of that asylum?? That too illegally?? You know what you're saying?" was Manju-bhai first reaction when I told him the 'help' that I needed.

"Yes Manju-bhai... Out of that bloody shithole... If that doesn't happen then I will never get rid of the restlessness in my mind..." I said and realised how I was still in deep shit of problems and how I was doing it more for myself than him. More to retain my sanity than to restore his.

But now I was determined and undeterred by the path that would lie ahead of me. I had dared to think straight and clear and had dared to keep looking that way without turning back... I had to do it. And had to do it all alone.

"Hmmm... Then only one guy can help you Ali..." Manju-bhai said smiling at me.

"Who? What's that smile?" I asked.

"Abdullah... Only he can help you now..." He said showing his beetle-teeth.

"What?? Abdullah? That asshole... He can help me in this?"

"Yes... The way you're saying that you need to get him out of some old building without permission... And you may have to bribe the security guard for that... Abdullah knows a lot of people around Bangalore and I tell you he can get it done..."

"Hmmm..." I grumbled in thought.

"But... How will you convince him? You've made him your biggest enemy…" Manju-bhai said huffing his trademark laugh.

"No… I'll talk to him… First you talk Manju-bhai… Don't laugh… If he can help then I'm ready to say sorry or whatever…" I said repenting my bad terms with Abdullah.

The skinny, dark Negro drug-supplier in the streets of Bangalore who would everyday supply those 'tiffin boxes' in all shady corners of the city. Manju-bhai too used to take hash and impure-marijuana from Abdullah to sell it to his fixed customers, some local laborers and road-side junkies.

My spat with Abdullah began when I once called his stuff impure and suggested a laborer that he can get better hashish in the city outskirts. Little did I knew the stubbornness of this crazy Negro drug dealer that from that day on, not a day passed that he would find me sitting in Sutta-point and would leave without saying atleast a word. I would obviously keep quiet and pretend to look unaffected, for I knew how strong his thin arms were. I knew a Negro punch can make me wet my pants.

"Ali… Abdullah will come tomorrow at 5.30 pm… Don't worry I'll talk… But you also be there…" he said and continued in a serious tone, "I've given my word that I'll help… Isn't that enough?"

"Well ya that is… You're a great person Manju-bhai…"

"Well that I know I am… Now you get going… Its 11.30… I've to sleep too…" he said patting my back.

"Ya… Sure…" I mumbled and climbed down the stairs. The door shut.

I glanced at the dark shutter-down Sutta-point in the night and raced the bike to hostel.

"Why do you come back so late nowadays? Where do you go *yar*?" Sandy asked as I entered the room.

"Just some small problem... I'll tell you sometime." I said pulling my shoe-laces.

He kept quiet.

"Sandy… I'm sorry to shout at you at times… You don't feel bad *na*?" I asked feeling terrible giving him airs.

"What? Hey… Are you… I mean… Are you on something? What did you take?" he asked suddenly raising his head.

"No… Nothing." I said in disgust.

"Oh! So you want some money is it?"

"No asshole… Ok I'm not sorry…" I said plunging into my bed.

After a pause he replied, "So how's Divya?"

Now this was Sandy. He didn't know the girl. He never cared to ask about her either. But here he was, asking me 'So how's Divya?' as if they've known each other since their diaper days.

"Ya… She's fine." I replied smirking at him. I knew this was the answer he expected. Not a dumb 'Hey how do you know her Sandy?'

"Tell her my hi okay… I hope you don't mind just one hi from me…"

"Ya… A small hi would be okay I think…" I said laughing and suddenly threw something towards him. The thing was my alarm clock… Bang!

"Okay good night… And at least show me her pic sometime you misery…" his voice came from under his blanket.

"Ya ya… We will go out together sometime… Good night…" I said talking to the blanket.

"Hah! finally aftr so many days… Gud nite… luv u:)" I sent her a message.

My eyes had no patience to wait for a reply. They shut down as my head dug into the pillow.

The day finally ended.

"He's asking me why aren't you talking yourself." Manju-bhai said as I reached the Sutta-point. Abdullah sat on one of the chairs, his eyes fixed on me.

"What's the matter mothafucka? So you need my help eh?" Abdullah said with a cunning smile. If it was dark, only his teeth would've been visible.

"Hmmm... Well ya... I do need your help." I said trying to ignore his irritating face.

"Why do you want someone out of NIMS Mental Asylum?" he said signaling towards a chair kept beside his table. That meant Abdullah was ready to talk. Good.

"Not the mental asylum... An old building that used to be the mental asylum... The people in that building are illegally confined... One happens to be my old friend..." I said trying to talk as straight as possible.

"And what do you expect from me?" he said again showing his toothpaste ad teeth.

"Well... Manju-bhai said you can help me in..."

"Fuck Manju-bhai... You tell me what you expect from me..." he cut me short.

"Well Abdullah... There's a guy in an old building in NIMS and he has to be rescued from there... From what I know, there's no legal way of doing that... But there's only one security guard at the building... Can you help me in anyway?" I said as Manju-bhai came and stood next to us.

After a cigarette lighting, first-puff and blowing the smoke pause, he said, "It's simple... Go at night... Beat up the guard... Get the guy..."

"No no no... That can be troublesome... We can bribe him... He's some old frail man I heard..." I said dreading the thought of Abdullah thrashing a helpless old man.

"Bribe him eh? That would be additional cost to you..." he said blowing more smoke.

"Additional?" I asked.

"Ya... Additional to my charges..." he said.

It was obvious that Abdullah would ask me for money. In fact that was the reason he was talking to me in the first place, as I was not some young black girl asking for help in this new city. But the thought stuck me now...

"Oh ya sorry... Your money... How much will that be?" I asked looking at Manju-bhai.

"That I'll tell you after the job... If it is all about beating up an old man, then why am I needed? Take Manju-bhai instead..." he said patting Manju-bhai's round tummy. He laughed his trademark laugh.

"No... I don't want to beat up any one Abdullah... Just wanna get him out of there silently..." I said giving Manju-bhai a stop-laughing look.

"And then..." he said.

"And then what?"

"And then do what with him?" he asked.

"Do what means what?" I asked puzzled.

"That means where will you keep him then mothafucka...?" he said yawning and stretched his body as he stood up.

I kept quiet.

Abdullah was right. An unbothered drug-supplier could think more logically than me. All these days I was thinking about heroic thoughts of rescuing Gopal out of those dark walls… But what next? What do I do with him once he was out of that room?

Maybe that's the reason people ended up in that room. When no one in the world was bothered about them, or turned back to ask about them, this was all the Government could do for such people … Pack them all in a single room and that's it. Feed them thrice a day and do whatever that kept them from dying and that's it. Hide their existence from any records and let them rot and that's it. That's how it is and that's it.

"Okay… I'll go now… Tell me when it is to be done…" Abdullah's voice jerked me from thought as he fled on his bike.

"See… I told you *na*… He will help you… This guy can get things done man…" Manju-bhai said smiling towards me.

I looked at him.

"What happened Ali? He's agreed no…" Manju-bhai said as the smile on his face disappeared.

"I don't know any place where he can stay Manju-bhai… Where will he go when he comes out? I'm totally fucked with this *yar*… One over another… The problems just don't end…" I said clutching my head tight with my fingers.

"Oh… You thought of that when Abdullah asked? What were you thinking Ali?" Manju-bhai asked.

"I've no idea what was I thinking and what am I thinking and whatsoever whosoever is thinking…"

"Again you're going mad… There will be some solution… We'll do something… Relax for now…" Manju-bhai said and patted my back.

He was smelling. Smelling of fried onions, of vinegar sauce, of a dirty USA shirt, of Sutta-point's kitchen, but also of a persistent and never-say-die spirit.

"Again… You'll have to help me with this Manju-bhai." I said looking at him.

"Nobody can help anyone Ali… Help always comes in forms… Be it me or you… Ultimately it's that Big Guy who's helping everyone…" he said pointing his index finger towards sky. Why do people think that God, if at all He exists, always stays in skies?

"Ya… I hope he's listening…" I said looking at the sunset. The sky's red and orange fusion got me lost into thoughts…

I knew it was some Puppet Show of some merciless Puppet Master. I knew there are snakes and they are left behind you by that same Master. They chase you while you run screaming for help, and that Master gets his entertainment dose by seeing your funny helplessness. No puppet can raise his voice against this Master, and when he does, his fellow puppets beat him up and tell him to shut his mouth and keep praising and pleasing the same Master that he wants to curse. *Just shut your mouth and keep praising and pleasing the Master.*

"Let's keep a time of two-three days… You also try and I too will try my best… You listening? Ali?"

"Ya… Ya I'm listening…" I mumbled and got up to leave.

"Okay… It's 7 pm… I'll go…" I said and left for the dinner-mess.

"One Lavazza…and…okay that's it", I told the waiter as I waited for Divya at the Brigades' Barista.

'thr in 10 mins… :)' my phone beeped with her text.

'fast fast fast...' I replied and the coffee arrived.

'hey im stuck with some work...wait for an hour more...plsss' her message appeared as I looked at the text helplessly.

"An hour more? What the fuck..." I got up whining and pushed back the coffee mug.

She stood in front of me.

"O...Oh my god..." I said and she took over...like always.

"What the fuck *eh*? You can't wait for me for even an hour is it?"

I held her shoulders, "Sorry sorry sorry... Sit... Sit down." I knew she could've easily lectured for an hour more, and a punch in front of that Barista crowd wasn't a good idea either.

"Looking good... " She said in the same snobbish tone, trying hard to curb a smirk.

"And you always look good..." I said taking her hand in mine.

And the usual talk began.

I looked around the Barista crowd for any signs of greenery. It was a dull but busy Sunday afternoon and the open air café was almost completely filled with good people. There were friends, boyfriends, girlfriends...old-friends. There were faces absorbed in books, faces looking around...faces absorbed in each other. Some *greenery* did prevail but Divya was easily the Miss Dull Sunday Afternoon Barista.

"See you anyway can't take him anywhere Ali. He has some mental disorder and that's why he's there. Only thing you can do is just get him shifted to the proper asylum building...the main one." She said as I told her my deep well of problems.

"But what difference will that make? Even that place would be the same..." I said keeping my head down on the table.

"No... Not at all... That place has much better amenities. Nice beds and food and all…we went there once on a behavioral analysis project…"

"And how does that happen? I mean how can I shift him there?" I asked looking up at her from the head-down posture.

"Even that is not simply possible…again you'll have to do something. Like I said… Contacts and stuff. And then even he might get a consideration for a treatment by the research department… There I can help… If he can really be cured you know…" she said as the coffee froth formed a white ring over her lips. I raised my hand and wiped it.

"I love you Divya…and I always want you to be by my side. When you smile at me…all the problems just fade off and life seems perfect for a moment." I said and rested my head on her palms. Her hand ran through my hair… She was addictive.

"Get up…come we'll walk…" she said and I suddenly took the scooty keys from the table.

"I'll ride today… Please… Just today…" I said slipping the keys in my pocket.

"You came by your bike you dumbo…otherwise you think I'll leave the keys in front of you like this. You have your bike today or else you had no choice but to sit behind preppy…" she said and blew air-kiss with fluttering eyelashes… Barbie dolls would have looked ugly as pigs in front of her at that precise moment.

After a usual long stroll at the Brigades', I bid her bye and rode my bike through the calm inroads of a relatively less busy afternoon Bangalore. I passed through the Hard Rock Café, Hotel Fanoos, The Forum…all these places had defined my life in the last five years in this city. I was a part of the crowd that I could see through my leisurely moving bike. I was a lost face in the big city crowd. I had my share of problems and my share of joys, my share of friends and my share of foes… I played a role in someone else's life…he played a role in mine. Life has to go on and life did go on.

It can be the either way – 'We live on' or 'Life goes on'…but it has to be some way.

Switching Sides

One month later.

"Results are gonna be announced soon I guess" Sandy said as he checked the University website on his laptop.

"You're anticipating results?? Fuck you…" I said going brutal on the last slice of pizza.

We sat in the same room no. 206 of BCE hostel. One month isn't a long time. Some things had changed and some hadn't…they never will.

Gopal existence had *switched sides*. Just the way Divya said. Abdullah told me to check the main asylum building one morning, I went and found Gopal roaming in clean clothes and a better looking face. His face was the same as it was once in the cycling ground…or to me it was the same.

Looking at him through the visitors' gallery window of the compound, I realised I missed him. Maybe he recognized me… but his mind is numb and non-verbal now. It doesn't react anymore. The doctor says he's calm and mute for life now. Maybe that's how it was written for him up there. I didn't feel sad for him…I just missed him…or just wanted to talk to him once.

Divya once said she'd do her behavioral analysis project on him. She saw him as a sample for a test or as Gopal, I didn't know…I didn't care. I was convinced that he was out of the dog's life. I passed him a chocolate bar or an ice candy at times through the window slit…before he could open the wrapper and start eating, I used to turn around and leave. Maybe I did care…but I tried hard not to.

"The semester exams are approaching. I suggest all of you all start studying now… The subjects this time are quite difficult." Iyer announced as I and Sandy sat on the last bench of the huge lecture hall.

"I haven't even bought some of the books yet… And he says start studying… Hah!" Sandy whispered and his mouth opened for a yawn. It got bigger and bigger…I felt like shoving whole of Iyer's body into it.

"Sandeep, what are you doing there? Stand up." Iyer's raised voice echoed through the silence.

Sandy got up rubbing his eyes. How much ever one would curse and cuss Iyer, one call from him in the classroom and no guy had the guts to stand up rubbing his eyes. But his twenty years experience of dealing with Government college brats bit dirt when it was Sandy. Sandy had the balls to look Iyer in the eye… And he was doing so now.

"Stand straight…keep your hands down *yar*…he's coming" I nudged him as Iyer angry face approached the backbench area.

"What was I teaching just now? Look here and answer mister…What was being taught just now?" Iyer screamed like a dog whose ass was set on fire.

"Hmm… Sir you were telling us to start studying early this semester… And that the subjects this time are…"

"Before that… I'm asking what I was teaching… Not this…" Iyer came forward and banged the book hard on the table. Sandy continued looking him in the eye.

"I don't know" he said.

"Why you don't know? What were you doing here man?" Iyer was going mad. Sandy I think just wanted that.

"I fell asleep sir" Sandy said expressionlessly.

"What?? Fell asleep?? Get out of the class… I knew you won't be able to answer… You can't answer… You can't stay… Get out…" Iyer said going back towards the podium. The fire in his ass extinguished as he finally found a reason to turn Sandy out.

"The term laser stands for light amplification by stimulated emission of radiation. Laser is a device that emits spatially coherent electromagnetic radiations through a process called stimulated emission…these were your last lines sir." Sandy roared through the silence as the whole class turned heads towards him hurriedly.

Iyer looked at him stunned. "Hmm… Ok… Sit down… Keep awake in the class… Sit down." he said after a moment, still stunned.

Sandy sat, grinning widely at me.

"Fuck… How did you know that?? Amazing *yar*… You shut him up." I whispered looking at his face.

"Keep it in your bag…" he said handling me a sheet of Iyer's notes.

"His notes? How did you get this copy?" I said folding the sheet of small as possible.

"That dumbass banged the book on the table and this paper fell out… His last read one… I just kept it down and read it as he went away." Sandy said and yawned again…

He never let himself down in front of Iyer and the legacy continued. Iyer was a dog and Sandy was right when he said, 'the name is an insult for the Sutta-point dog'.

That was Sandy's way of tackling the bullies that threatened to trespass into his free mind. In the eye and on the face. Be it Iyer or the night races with unknown bikers, Sandy had the same approach… Fuck you!

"So your exams are approaching again? When do you plan to start studying?" Divya said after almost a minute's silence that only had the sound of dry leaves crumbling under our feet.

"Oh my god… Now you too have started with this… C'mon…I'll study when I've to." I said trying to look unaffected by the scares of approaching majors.

"I'm just telling you… I know you and your roomie start studying only the night before."

"You can't believe how he waits till the eleventh last hour to lift the books… I'm not that complacent… I start off a bit early…" I said as we found a corner to sit for a while.

"Hmm… Do you have some cash right now?" she suddenly asked straightening up.

"Ya… hmmm… three hundred maybe…why?" I asked pulling out my wallet.

"So let's go somewhere!" she said with a sudden sparkle in her eyes.

"Somewhere? Where? It's 10 into the night…" I said trying to laugh off her sudden strange whim… I knew she was serious and there was no way out now.

"We'll come back by 11 or 12… Now get up fast…" She said pulling my hand.

"What? That'd be so late… No no… We'll go tomorrow Divya." I said still hoping that she might relent. Miracles do happen.

"Late? Shit man! Look at you. You're scared of the night? Don't worry I'll protect you... Anyone molests you in the public and I'll break his hand ..." she said giggling at me and ruffled my hair. I looked at her and smiled... that was all I could do.

"Wait here I'll come in a minute..." she said and disappeared into the women's hostel block.

Five minutes later she reappeared, same pajamas and tshirt, same loosely tied hair, just when I wondered what she had gone in for, I saw the scooty keys dangling in her hand.

"No no... Hey c'mon... I... I'm just not sitting behind you this time. Whatever happens... Not this time."

A minute later I found myself abruptly leaning backwards as the scooty jerked forward. I thought I would hold my ground this time and this was the result...I was trying to hold myself on to the lousy pillion seat... Miracles don't happen.

I slipped my hands into the warmth of her jacket as our chariot rolled out of the NIMS main gate. The night was foggy and numb-cold and anyone would be crazy to go out into the streets only to find with shutters down shops and stray dog packs. But here we were...out in the open.

"Where to? Everything seems to be dead." I said as a thick cloud of fog rolled out of my mouth.

"Everything's not dead... Some places are still alive. Shut up and sit." She said and that was probably the longest she'd have ever spoken while riding.

"Why are you turning towards Kormangala now?" I asked leaning forward, my nose almost numb from the chill. I knew I won't get an answer now and I didn't.

I looked around as the scooty slowed down and stopped into a busy young crowd.

We were at 'The Paramount', one of the few places in Bangalore that remained dead during the day and came alive as the day darkened.

As usual, people stood around in small groups, smoke rings fused into the fog and Marlboro smell mixed with the icy smell of the night.

She looked at me and smiled with twinkling black eyes. Black jacket, black pajamas and my black skull cap covering her head... She looked like a mysterious beauty made out of the night itself. I slipped her cold hand into mine and we walked in.

Paramount at night enclosed suave and sharp dressed gentry and her pajamas and loosely tied unruly hair caught a few whispering glances. More of them were from men who pretended to be unaffected by the stunning beauty who just entered... She insulted the place in her own smooth style, and managed to stand out in the crowd in which everyone looked the same.

"You know what? I'll try hookah today..." She said as I sank further into the ultra soft, ultra comfy couch.

"Hookah? Hah! You think you can smoke?" I asked looking at guy smoking Marlboro and wished I too could take a puff.

"Why? Why can't I smoke? Big deal... Order some hookah and anything to eat...fast!" she said reclining into the couch and leaned against me.

For a moment I thought, the night was dark and cold, she lived alone in the city, yet here she was on a night out with me without any second thoughts, leaning against me when she felt sleepy and smiling at me with those drowsy eyes knowing that I'll never betray her trust. She trusted me more than I myself did. I felt a sudden jitter on the thought of ever betraying her...I concentrated on the menu.

"Green apple hookah...hmm...and rest later" I told the waiter whose eyes wandered towards her bare feet on the couch.

"That's it for now." I repeated towards him and his eyes came back to my face…he left.

"Why did you come if you were so sleepy?" I said running my fingers through her thick hair. The dim yellow lighting and the fire of the candles reflecting in her eyes made her look ethereally beautiful…beyond words.

"I'm not sleepy preppy… When is the hookah coming?" she suddenly straightened up but her eyes remained the same, "Tell me if any guy is staring at you okay…" she said and giggled.

"They all are actually… They're wondering what this super-hot female is doing with this tall and lean guy." I said as she stretched out her legs on the couch.

"Not just tall and lean… Tall, lean and ugly. I'll forgive them… End of the day they're right." She said and hit me on the head with a cushion. I bent forward and kissed her cheek.

The hookah arrived and the waiter left…this time without wandering his eyes around.

"Take… Smoke up…" I said holding out the pipe in front of her.

"Don't look at it from all angles… Take it and smoke…" I said pushing it in her hand.

She sucked in the smoke as her eyes closed tighter and tighter and suddenly erupted in cough with white haze emerging everywhere on her face.

"Told you *na* you can't take it… Give it here." I said looking at her as tears pooled into her eyes.

I smoked in a thick chunk and tactfully formed smoke rings that rose above both of us.

"See this is how it's…"

Before I could finish my boss-talk, she snatched the pipe from my hand and suddenly sucked in more smoke than I ever could. Thick and dense rings gradually emerged out of her mouth as I looked at her my jaw dropped.

"Whoa! Divya... That's you??" I exclaimed in amazement as she smiled at me with watery eyes.

"This is how it's done..." She said and winked, "You couldn't beat me even in smoking dumbo."

Later chicken filled our stomachs and hookah smoke kept visiting our lungs. Fruit hookah was enough for her lungs to drowse her view as they had never experienced anything more than pure air. My lungs were a veteran...I only felt a sharp apple taste as I tongued my lips.

"Ali... Why is everything kinda rotating? Am I high?" She said unknowingly giggling while she talked.

"Yes you are. That too on fruit hookah." I said taking the keys from her pullover pocket, "I'm gonna ride now. Don't argue a word."

She smiled at me as her head rested deep into the soft leather recliner. I got up feeling the cold again climbing over my body and pulled her hard by the wrist.

"Get up... We'll leave." I said still holding her wrist. Her wrist was held in my fist and her eyes were looking into mine, the moment for a second took me back to that day in the local bus. Today, the wrist was same, the hand was same...but the times had changed. Today she wasn't struggling...she was smiling.

We walked out again into the cold night as thick fog and biting cold welcomed us from the doorway still crowded with people.

"Sit behind me." I said leaving her hand and climbed on the scooty.

"Can't believe I'm letting you drive." she said and tried to shove her little helmet onto my head.

"It won't fit me... You just sit. Sit fast or I'll freeze Divya. It's so fucking cold!" I said with battering teeth.

Finally I got to ride the scooty which had given me a world of embarrassment, but more than that a world that I cherished.

The city was dead dark at two am with a blinding white fog engulfing us both. I passed the sleeping gate keeper at the NIMS gate and stopped the scooty under a street lamp, feeling an urge to eat the fire in the bulb up there.

"I'll leave now... You too go. It's late..." I said getting down.

"What?" I asked seeing her expressionless face fixed at me.

"What?" I asked again waving my hand.

She lunged forward and our lips melted into each other.

All the cold suddenly drained out and the coziness of her body filled into me.

"I love you..." she said resting her forehead on mine.

Her voice had the drowsiness of the hookah and her body was loosening onto me. I held her straight and settled back the hair falling over her face.

"It's late now Divya...time to go. Ride to the hostel...take." I said passing her the keys.

"Bye..." She smiled at me as the scooty moved forward and instantly faded into the fog. I stood looking at the fading red tail lamp and wondered how she found reasons to love a person like me... a self-centered recluse with an unconcerned brain.

I killed the engine to avoid waking up the guard as the RX approached the hostel.

"Open the door. I'm standing outside...fast!" I said as a sleepy Sandy picked the phone.

After numerous similar calls, the door opened and probably the only man in Bangalore wearing just boxers stood in front of me.

"Where were you? It's fuckin three am man." He said in a creaking voice adjusting his eyes to the sudden light.

"Fuck! You still wearing only boxers. How are you alive?" I said wondering how a stark bare body could survive the night's chill.

"I'm alive. You are dead…" He said going back into his blanket.

"I'm dead? Why?" I casually asked taking a Navy-Cut stick from the pack kept alongside his pillow.

"You're dead coz the results are out you moron. Where were you? You've got four backs." His voice rose from underneath the blanket.

"W H A T !!!" the cigarette dropped from my lips and a killing darkness erupted inside my head.

"Whhaaaat did you just say?" I asked as my eyes probably hung out of the sockets.

"The results came out Ali. I'm sorry but you've to face it… You've failed in four subs." He said coming towards me and picked the cigarette up from the floor.

I looked at his face unable to say what I wanted to… An iron rod would have rammed through my chest and I wouldn't have felt a thing.

"Why so serious?" Sandy said getting his face inches close to mine and burst out laughing.

"Look at your face. You seem fucked in and out. I was kidding *yar*. The results are not even out yet." He said and sat next to me resting his arm on my back.

"ffffuck you man!" I said jerking his hand off, "I don't know how to kill you."

"You can't kill me. Ever seen such muscles before." He said flexing his biceps, I had to agree his push-ups routine was finally showing results.

"Get off my bed... I'm super sleepy..." I said digging my head into the pillow and trying to forget what I had just gone through.

"Where were you? Divya?" he asked going to his bed.

"Yes." I said and pulled up the blanket.

"Night out? Where?" he asked.

"Nothing much... Went to Paramount. Rest in the morning *yar*... Please." I said almost switching off.

"You are one lucky ass you know... Good night." He said and went into the blanket.

'You are one lucky ass...' his words suddenly opened up my eyes. I knew he was right.

The chill of the night and the warmth of her lips went through my mind. The soft recliner at the Paramount and her head resting on me, the waiters' eyes fixing on her bare feet and her watery eyes after the long hookah puff...all the images went through my mind as my eyelids came closer and closer.

Finally...Sleep.

Reality Bites

"The results are out *oye*!" Happy Singh suddenly appeared and disappeared from the ajar door.

"Did he just say that the results are out?" I asked Sandy hysterically getting up from the bed.

"Hmmm... Ya... It sounded quite like that." Sandy said staring blankly at me.

"Fuck! Then run..." I said running out and Sandy followed slamming the door behind him.

"Where you going? Let's check the University site..." he asked catching up with me as I rushed down the hostel stairs.

"Site will be busy... I'm going to the college notice board" I said running as my terribly scarce stamina started giving way.

"What the fuck! Are all those guys so eager to see the results?" Sandy said as we watched a mob of people going violent in front of the notice board. Some scanning the long hanging result papers, some just being pushed back and trying again.

"You go and check mine too..." I said trying to make it look easy.

"I'll check mine...Not yours" Sandy said and fused into the crowd.

"Just check it whether I have at least passed in all..." I called out.

Standing near the notice board waiting for their results to be read out, one probably lives the longest minutes of his college life... Dark, full of pictures, and the most fucked up longest minutes.

Sandy suddenly emerged out from the crowd and pushed me hard to the ground.

"What? What happened?" I said as my butt landed on the cold marble.

"What the fuck Ali! What the fuck!" he exclaimed raising me up and hugged me hard, almost breaking my ribcage.

Suddenly the crowd of people at the notice board started approaching me and a series of congratulatory handshakes started.

"Congrats *yar* Ali."

"Amazing man. How did you do it? Congrats."

"Unbelievable! What a brilliant result!"

I ran to the notice board and scanned the sheets for my name.

"92.22 % - University Rank 1" I read the digits as my vision blurred.

"Oh man oh man!" Sandy said and again hugged me as the crowd kept looking at us, "How did you do it Ali? You surpassed all those nerdy girls in the class man..."

"What's happening..." I unknowingly murmured in the lowest possible tone.

"What what's happening? Can't you see? You got the first rank in the University Ali! That's like the best crap in the history of this college..." He said struggling to find an appropriate expression to react.

"First rank in the University? Me?" I thought or I said...I couldn't make out.

Suddenly a blurred canvas of faces started revolving around my head.

Mom, dad, Raghu, Sandy, Divya, Manju-bhai and even Gopal... All shouting praises at me as their voices fused into each other.

I shut my ears hard to the disturbing melee of sounds as their intensity raised higher and higher.

Suddenly the ringtone of my cellphone muted all of them and pierced through my eardrums.

BOOM... The dream was over.

I woke up sweating as I looked around the room. The cellphone was ringing for real.

"I'll call you later" I told Divya and adjusted out of the megalomaniacal fantasy.

Sounds of snores droned out of blanket lump on the other bed. I gulped down some water from the bottle kept on the side table and wiped the cold sweat off my forehead.

I bit my lower lip slightly to confirm that the dream was really over... The sensation assured that reality had kicked in... *Coz Reality Bites.*

'results out' I reached the room after college hours when the message beeped.

I blankly looked around to check if it was a sequel to the mornings' dream when suddenly Sandy's heavy hand patted my back as he entered the room...It wasn't.

"True that the results are out?" I said dropping my bag.

"Ya... I too heard." Sandy said trying hard to flex his abs...there weren't any.

"Then let's go to the college and check...Fuck! I'm scared." I said as Sandy's forceful flexing resulted in a noisy fart...still no abs.

"The result won't be displayed in college. Check it on the site..." he said smiling and let out another.

"Shit! Stop farting you ass... The results are out! You aren't getting scared?" I said and typed the University site address.

"You know what? I try hard but I just don't get that result tension *yar*... How do you get this super hot tension and all? Give me some tips no..." he said going into the push-ups position.

"You'll work out right now? Fuckin results are out here and you can work out... You're right. You need some medical treatment to get tensed." I said refreshing the site.

"Medical treatment? Oh... You know any doctor? I mean any nice neurosurgeon...or to be neurosurgeon? That will also do." He said and winked at me from the floor.

"Fuck you! Do the push-ups now if you really have the balls..." I said and sat over his back.

He made a screeching sound and lifted whole of my body in one intense jolt of force... A wide grin ran across his reddened face as I looked at him jaw-dropped.

The evening grew darker and the result wave spread across every corner of the hostel now. More than half of the dorm gallery gathered in room no. 206, all waiting for the site to do anything more than just refresh.

"Oye it's opened!" Happy Singh erupted as if Angelina Jolie just emerged open in front of him.

The roll numbers started entering in and I patiently waited for my turn on the only laptop that managed to get more than just refresh out of the sadistic site.

The longest minutes' period started for me as I looked at good and bad results appear on the screen. I thought of the morning dream and visualized whole of the crowd suddenly turning towards me with handshakes and hugs.

"Whooo... Ali... 68 %" A voice came out from the crowd.

"Who?? Me?? 68??" I said pushing aside people to reach the screen.

'Uh! So here it is? 68.' I murmured sinking in the reality and confused feelings of joy and sadness came around to surround me. Joy that I hadn't flunked in any…Sadness because human expectations never sub due.

"68!! Party party party…" Sandy said trying to hang behind my back.

"Get off!! How was your's?" I asked turning around.

"65 not out!!" he said and tried to do something that he thought was dance.

I looked around the room pushing aside his ugly moving figure from my sight.

Happy was *happy,* the ever smiling surd had managed a monstrous 72, I smiled at his hairy grinning face and felt a terrible guilt for a second.

The more people I asked around, the more insignificant my 68 became. Some were calling home and others were switching off their cellphone to avoid the same. I knew I didn't have the second option, I had to tell dad.

"Dad… Hmm… The results are out." I said trying to pitch in the sadness in my voice that I rehearsed fifteen times before calling.

"Oh the results? How was your's *Ali*? What's the top percentage?" Dad asked.

Top percentage??? I thought of shouting 'hello hello' and disconnecting.

"Ali… You there? How was the result?"

"I… I got a 68 dad. And the highest is nowhere even close to it."

"Hmmm… Nice nice… Good… 68 is good. Don't worry…" Dad said with same care and concern in his voice that he didn't require to rehearse like me…but I knew it was fake…He had asked the top percentage first.

"I'll talk to you later" I said and cut the call before I would've heard the same cajoling words from mom.

Looking out of the window, I visualized mom and dad's face as the damp wind combed through my hair. I knew they wanted me to do better...To be a better rat in this world of maddening rat race. I knew I had thousands around me who were a thousand times better than me... But I was mom and dad's champ and they made sure never to let me feel otherwise.

"What you doing here? Come let's go to the senior wing..." Suddenly Sandy's face appeared in front of me jerking me out of thought.

"N... Nothing... Nothing. Why senior wing? What happened?" I asked settling my hair.

"Don't you know? Raghu... He topped the college man... Some University rank too I guess... Let's just go and congratulate him once." He said pulling me.

"Raghu? Again? Amazing. But you go... I won't come. I'll talk to him later." I said and went out of the room.

'congrats yar...n hope you remember me??' I messaged Raghu and fired the RX.

'im coming...there in 10 min' I messaged Divya and raced the bike away from the dark result world.

"Why did you come suddenly? That too so late? What if the night *goondas* had eve-teased you..." she chuckled as I got down.

"Bad result." I said looking blankly at her face.

"Oh...that's why you decided to come eh? So that you get pacified out of your sadistic engineering life..."

"Sadistic is an understatement..." I said removing my helmet, "It's so damn chilled here... Isn't there any closed place in the campus that'd be open now?"

"Closed place?? Open now?? Hmmm… Come let's go…" She said holding my cold palm in hers.

We walked into the bushy inroad of the NIMS Campus and entered the 24-hour cafeteria in the Emergency block.

"What's the smell?" I said as I looked around the huge hall filled with empty chairs and tables.

The ambience of cafeteria could've well qualified for a mournful obituary ceremony. Dull eyes of waiters looked at us as we found a corner to sit.

"So… How bad is the damage?" She said sitting on the chair opposite to mine.

"68 percent bad." I said and gasped.

"Oh shit! You didn't flunk in any subject. Bad…" She said laughing, "Remember I said once…You're gonna flunk if you keep visiting me like this. So your result isn't that bad you see."

She put a smile on my face and I got what I came for…Her smile.

The night had deepened as I rode into the BCE campus, unable to see the hostel building eaten up by fog.

'thanks yar… n don't be silly… i hvnt forgotten u… jus been a lil busy…' I read Raghu's message getting off the bike.

"Open the door goddamnit!" I screamed as I stood outside knocking hard for the tenth time.

The door opened… 'WHAT…THE…FUCK!!!' I shouted taken aback by the scene inside.

Six bodies lay randomly on the floor. Those who looked like my classmates couple of hours ago were now unrecognizable wasted drunkards.

"Welcome to the result paaaarty..." Sandy said trying hard to say what he wanted to.

"Result party uh?" I said walking across the room.

Empty bottles and soon to be empty bottles spread across the floor. Sandy and Happy were the only ones with open eyes...rest had passed out.

Unconscious bodies of Mayank and Kumar lay on the two beds. Surender and Virender lay knocked out on the floor...as always on each other.

"Catch... Get sloshed!" Sandy tossed a Old Monk rum bottle into my hands.

"You know that I don't drink..." I said towards him and realized it was impractical to make him understand anything right now.

I went to the loo and found it was no more the same loo...it was a puke-yard.

"Fuck! Who all puked in there?" I asked running out as Sandy and Happy just looked at me and smiled.

"Okay what the fuck is happening? What party is this? Get up and go wild!" I asked switching on the woofers to the max and shook up the passed out figures to life.

"Whooooo..." Sandy got up and gulped in a heavy swig from his beer bottle.

"Okay... Pass me a joint." I smirked at Sandy and the 'result party' was alive again.

"Oye Ali... How's your *gullfryand yar*?" Happy asked as I rolled out the thick marijuana smoke from my mouth.

"What girlfriend? I don't have any." I said looking at the rings rising up in the air.

"Oye don't fool me *yar*... I'm talking about the *gullfryand* you have at that NIMS College..." he said putting his arm around me.

"What the fuck! Who told you this now?" I asked him startled... He smiled at Sandy. Sandy smiled at me.

"Get me also some *gullfryand* yaaaar..." Happy said further tightening his arm around me.

Ever since puberty hit him, Happy Singh is in a desperate search of a *gullfryand*... And I know it will remain the same until an *ishtylish* Punjabi wedding comes to his rescue. The happy surd had tried it all...from regional chat rooms to random pick-up lines at pubs that sometimes even got the bouncers involved. But the only set of naked boobs he ever got to see never came out of the computer screen...if Kumar's male breasts are not taken into counting that is.

"I'm hungry... Who else?" I said looking at everyone as Happy's heavy head with long open hair lay sloshed on my lap.

"I'm not... I'm full with booze..." Sandy said drowsily.

I had smoked enough marijuana to feel the familiar extreme urge of hogging unlimited food and gulping down glasses of water.

"Party over... Now port these bodies to their room somehow..." I told Sandy shoving a scoop of the just cooked Maggi into myself.

Sandy maxed the volume on the woofers and I opened the window to let the icy fresh wind of the night replace the marijuana-booze infested air of the room.

Pink Floyd's 'Time' piped into my ears...

'And you run to catch up with the sun but it's sinking.

Racing around to come up behind you again.

The sun is the same but you're older.

Shorter of breath and one day closer to death.'

Here we were, I thought as I looked around the room, a bunch of engineering college graduates on a 'result party' that was actually a drunken brawl… and on a *unconcerned* journey that was actually life.

With booze blessing our livers and marijuana blessing our lungs… We had the song of life on our lips…and four years of it to kill.

Flames to dust… Lovers to friends…

24th Dec 2008 - 1800 hrs – Room no 206 – Situation: Pretty fucked up.

"Micro-Processors' lab is day after tomorrow man… I better start now… When you gonna start studying?" I asked Sandy as I analyzed my impossibly cluttered study table from all angles…wondering whether it would be practical to think about clearing all that mess successfully.

Exam season had prevailed again in the BCE hostel. Study tables started unloading the crap they mounted up the whole semester… Human brains started in-loading the crap the notes mounted up the whole semester.

"Hah! You think you can clear all that mess yourself? Get a bulldozer…" Sandy said opening the overweight MP book, "Thirty programs… All look like ancient sculptures… Where does one start in this?"

"I don't know? I'm gonna start today… Do hell with the logic and all… I'll just mug…" I said and stationed myself onto the bed. Table mess will need a bulldozer.

"Oh! Full determined uh? What about this message on your phone?" he said and threw the phone on my bed.

'i got a couple entry pass to inferno… i know its stupid to ask u as ur exams r up… but still... buzz me if u can come or I'll hv to go wid another fren…' – Divya.

"When did this come?" I asked looking at him.

"Fifteen minutes ago… Just before you entered..." Sandy said, "So you still determined to study eh?"

"Ya! I'll sit and study *yar*…" I said keeping the phone aside and looked deep into the modern sculptures of MP programs.

"Inferno, it's the best fuckin disc in whole of Bangalore man… You've seen the babes that come there?? Think of it Ali!" Sandy said walking towards me, "MP exam you can write next sem also… But a free entry to Inferno that too on the Christmas eve… I can fuckin murder you to get in there if given a chance…"

"Next sem?? You want me to get a back for this lousy disc or whatever… Fuck off!! I'm trying hard to concentrate man…" I said shifting my mind out of the babes-laden dark atmosphere of the Inferno… It wasn't lousy.

"Chill! You won't flunk… We've got tomorrow to study… And didn't you see the message? She'll go with someone else if not you… Who's this someone else?" Sandy said as I read the message again.

"You sure it's some someone and not someONE??" he continued with his grinning face.

'im comin' I replied to the message.

"And I'm coming too…" Sandy said peeping in the screen from behind.

"Where you gonna go?" I asked.

"Party at my farmhouse. I know… Doesn't sound as cool as Inferno. But the food's gonna be amazing… And I'll see mom and dad too… It's been long…" he said and patted my back, "Get up and change now…fast! Fuck the exams… Whooooo…"

I bathed in deodorant to compensate for the last two days I had spent without a bath. I had a reason… Chilling cold. Sandy had to bathe longer as in his case it was six days…he didn't need a reason.

"Drop me there… that gate…" I said pointing at the NIMS main gate as the RX slowed down.

"How will you travel to Inferno by the way? It's far from here… Mysore Road…" he asked as I got down.

"I'll go by…" I said suddenly pausing at the thought of the scooty ride, "umm… It's okay… I'll go somehow…"

"Okay bye… Have fun with Inferno babes you lucky ass… While I try to combat all those ultra rocking oldies gathered at my place…" he said and sped ahead leaving me alone in the dark.

'wr r u? come soon… im waitin near d asylum building…' The phone beeped.

Asylum Building… the words sent a jitter down me and I jerked my head to get off the sudden lump formed within.

'Divya… You come near the main gate… I'm waiting here…' I said as she picked up on the other side. Before she could reply, I cut the call. I wish certain things in life too could be just *cut off* on one press of a button…before they could reply.

I looked at the dark image of her approaching scooty as it emerged from the foggy inroad.

"Oh my god! What are you wearing Ali!" She said braking hard in front of me.

"Why what's wrong?" I asked looking down and confirmed I hadn't forgotten the pants back in the room.

"We're going to Inferno… Not CCD… It's the Christmas bash there… And you're in your regular jeans and pullover…" she said laughing at me and removed her helmet.

"So you think…" I suddenly stopped. The words in my mouth froze as I looked at her awestruck.

Red lip-rogue shone on her smile adorned lips under the dim street light. Golden tan on her flawless face and dusky kohl in her deep black eyes… The spark in her aura was intense enough to set me burning into flames right there.

"What!!" She asked and bought me to life.

"Nothing… It's just that you look so ugly…" I said and hopped onto the pillion seat.

"Don't worry… I can never beat you on that…" She chuckled and we set out for Mysore Road.

Sharp smell of her perfume blew past me as she sped through the long deserted stretches at night. Sitting behind jobless, I compared my rugged pullover and jeans to her suave party-wear clothing… She was dressed for Inferno, I for the roadside *chai*-shops that went past us.

"Stop stop stop… Stop before that crowd…" I said as we approached the people standing outside this suppose-to-be most happening place in Bangalore.

"Why here??" She asked stopping with a screech.

I instantly got down, "You go and park… I'll come walking till there…"

Jumping out of the pillion seat of a girlish scooty wasn't very smooth a move to attract the attention around.

We walked in and as usual the smell of smoke and cocktail greeted us into the dark atmosphere. I looked around as my eyes adjusted to the faint lighting… There were girls under layers of paint and guys with pointed set of shoes desperate to express their sharp dressing sense. But all that didn't make much of a difference as nobody noticed nobody…

Had I entered dressed like Santa Claus and then may have got a few glances. Divya was anyways getting them… I could've entered stark naked and wouldn't have managed so many.

"A-a-a-and where does one sit here?" I said scanning the long row of couches filled with people.

"Why do you need to sit? You didn't come here to sit preppy… You'll have to dance…" She said pulling me to the other side.

"What?? Dance??" I whined… getting ignored completely.

Blaring music tore through my ears as she pulled me into the disc area. It was loud and dark… Loud so that nobody talks, dark so that everyone goes blind… Shut your mouth and don't look around… Just dance - the place said.

"I won't dance…" I said trying to get off her grip. I could've… But I let her hold on.

"I can't dance to save my life Divya… Come we'll sit somewhere…" I said as we moved away from the blindness and deafness. I was determined that I wouldn't dance and knew all along that ultimately I'll have to.

I moved into the cluster of people trying to find a foothold on the crowded dance floor. All my life whenever I came to nightclubs, I laughed at the people dancing on the floor and wondered what one got out of it… But here I was today standing amidst those very same people. Being stupid ceased to matter, being laughed at ceased to matter… She mattered.

I tried to do something that wouldn't even remotely look like dance. The revolving flash lights around made her face switch on-off in front of me. I knew I looked worse than Sandy in those moments, but her hand in my hand and the darkness around us made the 'dance' ordeal look worthwhile.

'Flames to dust… Lovers to friends… Why do all good things come to an end…'

I swayed along with the music, my arms around her waist and the fragrance of her perfume mellowing into me… I wished Nelly Furtado was wrong… I wished all good things never came to an end and all the bad ones did… That the flames never became dust and lovers remained lovers.

"So this was it *uh*? The place which might even make me flunk my exams… In-fer-no." I said reading the electrified letters displayed outside the doorway.

It was 10 pm into the night, the music had numbed my ears and to break away from the smoky air inside, we escaped to the serene air of the lawns.

"Who asked you to come? Anyways I could've gone with someone else…" She said smirking at me.

'You sure it's some someone and not someONE??' Sandy's grinning face flashed for a second and I suddenly asked, "And who's this someone?"

"Hmmm… There is someone… a friend of mine…" she said walking ahead.

"It was a couple entry I guess? Who's this friend? You never told me…" I asked abruptly stopping.

"Told you? Why should I tell you? I don't have to tell you everything…" She said looking back and kept walking, "His names Tenzin by the way…"

"Divya? Is there a problem?" I said feeling lost in the vastness of the night.

She walked upto me and said with a stern face, "Yes, there is a problem Ali…"

I looked at her blankly, "What problem?"

"The problem's that Tenzin is my roomie…" she said and burst out laughing.

"Your roomie? Hah! You were talking about a goddamn girl?" I said looking at her smiling face under the moonlight.

"Yes… A goddamn girl you dumbo… And look at your face…" She said and ruffled my hair.

We walked together on the wet grass away from the voices inside the discotheque. Sandy was wrong, the babes-laden Inferno wasn't the best place to be on this Christmas-eve… I could've killed a hundred such Infernos for one moment of this moonlit walk.

"Why did you ask all those questions? You don't trust me if I tell you I'll go out with a friend?" She asked as I got down from the scooty in front of BCE Campus.

'Damn Sandy' I thought for a moment.

"Hmmm… It's not the trust… It's just that I've been lucky enough to find someone like you… And now I can't be dumb enough to lose that…"

She looked at me and smiled, "Bye preppy…" She said and sped off.

"Bye…" I mumbled to myself and started the long walk from main gate to the hostel.

It was getting harder to love Divya, I thought as I walked… For the first time I was trying dance in a disc knowing that it wasn't dance, for the first time I was tossing my books away on flash of one message, for the first time my eyes were looking more into the eyes of a girl than anything else.

It was easy to pretend love when it wasn't… But it was hard to live with it when it really was.

"What up…!" Sandy's hard hand hit my back as he skid the RX before me.

"You coming now? How was the party?" I asked sitting behind and soothed my back...*Damn those push-ups.*

"Same old boring... You tell me... How were the bare legs and plunging cleavages at Inferno?"

"Inferno??" My mind went back to her bare feet on wet grass, "You were right *yar*... Inferno is the best place to be..."

"Hail Sandy!!" He screamed into the silence of the night.

"Ali! Where are you?" Something spoke to me in deep sleep.

"Ali... ALI!!!" The speaker of the phone blasted.

"Huh! D...D...Divya. What happened?" My mouth asked. Rest of me still sleeping.

"Come to NIMS... Now..." She said from the other end.

"Now?? So early in the morning?? Let me sleep..." I said half woken up.

"Early?? It's 11... Ali! Get up and see the time... I'm waiting here. Come soon." She disconnected and suddenly whole of me woke up.

I looked outside the window and stretched. The sun was shining sharp...what better job he had.

"Get up..." I said to the blanket on the other bed.

"11 o clock... Merry Christmas... And merry tomorrows MP lab..." I said shoving in the minty toothbrush as Sandy emerged.

"Hey Divya... What's the matter?" I asked on the phone.

"You have still haven't left?? Come fast..."

"Anything important? Coz I've a lab exam tomorrow... And I can try passing that if I manage to place my ass on the chair for twelve hours straight from now... I think I'll give it a try..."

"Ali… Don't kid… Can't tell it on the phone… I'm serious… Please come..." she said cutting me short.

"Hmmm… Okay." I cut the call. I always knew I had to go.

"I'll come in… hmmm… an hour…" I told Sandy and slammed back the door.

"Come soon… Don't forget the ghost called MP lab…" I heard him say.

I entered the NIMS Campus and looked around for her. She wasn't there.

"Where are you?" I asked as she picked up on the other end.

"You came? I waited for you there…" She said speaking softly.

"Ya I came… And why are you speaking so low?"

"I'm amongst some people and…"

"Listen Divya… If you can show up in a couple of minutes then great otherwise I better leave… I've to study loads and wishing each other Christmas isn't that important… You're gonna come or we'll meet tomorrow? Tell me fast." I asked frustrated.

"Ali! Listen to me… I didn't call you to wish Christmas goddamnit… I know you got an exam tomorrow but please do as I say…"

"Do what?" I asked interrupting her. *I too know I've an exam tomorrow, and only knowing doesn't help in my case, I have to study too.*

"Check the campus map… Come to the Neurology Department... Third room on the second floor…"

"WHAT???" I exclaimed, "You want me to do what? Come where?"

"Ali listen… Neurology Department… Come fast and call me…" she said whispering.

"Hey hey hey… Hold on… Divya… What's going on? What is it?" I asked helplessly.

She paused for moment and said, "Ali… Relax… It's about Gopal… Come fast I'm waiting here…"

Her words blew the daylights out of me… I couldn't relax.

You can run but not for long

"Were you serious?" I asked reaching the compound of the huge building.

"You think I'm kidding… Come with me... Fast!" She said and turned back into the doorway. I followed reluctantly.

People went up and down the long corridors. Some walked on legs…some on wheel chairs. The place was weary and gloom dripped from every face… And probably the last place one would want to be a day before 'the ghost called MP lab'.

"Divya… Will you stop and tell me your stupid reason for why I'm here..." I asked trying to keep pace with her fast steps.

"Enter and you'll know the stupid reason yourself…" She said halting before a door.

'Dr. Verma – Head, Neurology Dept.' I read the doorplate.

"What the fuck! Why are you going in?" I asked vainly following her inside.

The creature sitting inside stared at me as I entered… the expletive didn't go well with him.

I went and sat on one of the chairs and looked around the room. The same creature appeared in every single frame that hung on the walls, gleefully collecting awards in all stage of his life… from a thick hairy bush to a mirror shining bald.

"Hello young man… The names Ali right?" His hoarse voice echoed through the room.

"Hmm... Shake hands... Ali!" Divya nudged me as I found myself blankly staring at him.

"Ya... Hi...hi... Ali" I said feeling my hand lost into his pudgy paw.

"Hi... Doctor Sudhir Verma..." he said with an almost violent hand shake, almost biting look, "Welcome to NIMS..."

'Welcome to NIMS???' I can take you to corners that you thought never existed in NIMS you douche-bag panda, I want to tell him.

"Thanks... What's the matter?" I asked.

"Well... I'm running out of time so let's wrap this up as early as possible... So tell me... What Ms. Divya says is true?" He asked leaning forward. His moustache was older than me.

"And wh-h-h-at did Ms. Divya say?" I asked switching my view from his ugly face to her, well, pretty face.

"There's an inmate in the mental asylum... She says he was once your friend..." he shot his words at me.

A pair of steel hands closed around my windpipe. I waited for the grip to loosen...

"Ye...Yes... So? He once was... I think he..."

"Well that's enough for me to know... She'll tell you the rest... I gotta rush..." He cut short my stammering and went past us out of the room.

"What's going on Divya? What the fuck is going on?" I erupted as he left.

"Ali... Listen to me... Gopal's case is being taken up here... They say he can be cured..."

"What?? Cured??" I said standing up. I wanted to say more...to her and to the potbellied doc. Wanted to tell him to cure his hair loss instead and get a life... and wanted to tell her to leave me alone...for once.

But more than that I wanted fresh air away from the closing in walls of the room… I rushed out.

"Ali… What's wrong with you?" She asked following me.

"What's wrong? You tell me what's going right here? Infact just tell me what's going on here?" I asked trying not to look around the long corridors…filled with emptiness.

"Okay listen… I'll tell you the whole thing…" She said with a grim face, "I never let you know but I had put forward Gopal's case file in the neurology department… I had many seniors and all preferring it to all the docs available… and finally after such long efforts… it has been taken up here… that means NIMS finds an experimental treatment pragmatic… Now you understood?"

I looked at her blankly, "Damn your NIMS and damn Gopal man…" I said trying to keep sane with all her words surrounding me, "You know I've my exam tomorrow and you called me for this crap?"

"Crap? Ali this isn't crap? This is a question of someone's life goddamnit… And I called you in all hurry coz doctor Verma isn't so easily available you know… He's the head surgeon here… We had to meet him today or again it was a month long wait… You getting it?" She stopped seeing my blank face.

"Yes I'm getting it very well… And here is my part… Whatever you and your doctor Verma wants to do with him… Go ahead do it… Don't tell me and don't bug me… You people do great deeds by saving a life and all while I try to pass a lousy exam… Now you getting it?" I said trying to look hard into her eyes… I couldn't.

"Hah! Don't tell me and don't bug me is it?? This is all I expected from you Ali… And I never wanted to tell you all this either… But only if it was possible… This whole treatment and the dates… Nothing is possible without you Ali… Everything is in your hands…"

"What the fuck! In my hands?? Why me??" I asked puzzled.

"Because there is an undertaking goddamnit... Undertaking on the outcome of the surgery... Only you can sign it Ali... Not me not anybody... Only you... Doctor Verma met you for this only... You sign it and it happens... Please understand Ali... His life's dependent on you..."

She kept speaking while I looked at her with mute ears. I wanted water. I wanted new air. I wanted to wake up on my bed...

It didn't happen. It didn't end. I had to end it...

"Listen Divya..." I said trying to look away from her, "There's something you should know... I've gone through enough of shit because of this... And now I don't wanna look back... I don't care whatever medical wonders these fake assholes are trying to produce... I just don't care... I've tried hard to stay away from this and now please don't screw it up for me... I love you and that matters more than anything else ever did... I'll see you tomorrow... Never again bring this up... So I better leave now? It's afternoon..."

She kept her eyes fixed on me, "Never again bring this up?? I suggest you never again talk to me Ali... I too love you but not for the shallowness you're portraying right now. You're not what you're trying to be... You do care for him and whether you accept it or not, you can't change it... And that's precisely the reason you can't sign you know... Call me if you can manage to get off this pretence and do the right thing... Otherwise have a good time running away..." She said and walked back without turning once.

I could've done without the speech. I wanted to ignore her words. I wanted to think it was happening... I wanted to leave.

Tired and frustrated, I returned to the hostel room... expecting the sculptures of Micro Processors Lab to replace all her words haunting inside my head.

"Forget it!" Sandy said just as I entered.

"Forget what?" I murmured.

"Even the passing thought of passing… Hah!" he said with a same irritating grin.

"I don't wanna pass…" I said and collapsed into the bed.

"What?? Don't wanna pass?? No I was just kiddin… Actually we…"

"Fuck you! Shut up! I don't wanna pass… Lemme sleep…" I said and dug my face deep into the pillow.

Tranquility prevailed.

'This is a question of someone's life goddamnit…'

'Don't tell me and don't bug me…'

'Everything is in your hands… His life's dependent on you…'

'Never again bring this up…'

'I suggest you never again talk to me Ali… Have a good time running away…'

My eyes suddenly opened to a clangor of voices and images. With a wet forehead and a dry throat, I looked around the room.

For a change Sandy sat and not slept on the other bed… A fat familiar looking book lay under his gaze.

"What's that?" I said adjusting to the brightness.

"What's what?" he asked suddenly looking at me.

"That book you're reading… Which one?"

"Microprocessors… I wanna pass…" he said and turned back to the book.

I hysterically turned to the clock… 11 pm.

Reality kicked in… And so did panic, fear, shock and a shit loosening horror.

"The lab's tomorrow!! How I slept so long?? Why the fuck you didn't wake me??" I shouted jumping out of the bed.

"What?? Are you out of your mind?? You said you wanna sleep and don't wanna pass... Fuck you and shut up!"

"What!!"

"Even that you said..."

"Okay chuck that... teach me all the programs... fast!" I went and sat beside him trying to make the 'teach me all the programs' part look easy... It wasn't easy... It was impossible.

"What?? You know what you're saying?? Teach?? I'm not Raghu..." he said looking into the sculptures.

I wished he was Raghu. Or I wished Raghu was there. With Raghu it was possible...it somehow was. But times had changed... seeing Raghu was impossible.

"So what's the sum-up of this fuck-up??" I asked Sandy leaning on the backrest. I had to accept the inevitable. A first fail experience of my life was written ahead.

"Hmmm... the sum-up is that you're very intelligent... you had a good sleep at least... coz even if you'd have sat all evening... it'd have been useless... just as I'm trying to shove it in from time immemorial... and I'm still not thorough with even a single program..." he said lighting a fag.

"By the way what happened in the afternoon?? You looked quite fucked up... You just came and dozed off instantly..." he said looking at me.

I watched him blankly.

"What??" he asked again.

"Nothing happened... Pass one cig here." I called out...before the voices struck.

"I've an idea to pass tomorrow..." Sandy suddenly interrupted into my fragile concentration on the book.

"What idea??" I asked getting up and keeping the book aside... The fragility gave way.

"Sounds insane... But will work..." he said thinking into the air.

"What's the idea?? Nothing's gonna work now *yar*... The screw is ready for me up there... It's just waiting for the morning... How much ever I study... I won't be able to write the perfect error free code on the comp and get the output... I'm dead..." I said trying to sound relaxed. Trying to sound unconcerned. But the long dead nerd in me wasn't letting that happen... He shouted to be rescued alive.

"Hmmm... The idea... Here it is... Take a look yourself..." he said and tossed the Navy-Cut box into my hand.

"What the fuck do I do with this now?" I asked and opened the box... There were no cigarettes... There was a pen-drive.

I looked at his grinning face.

"Are you fuckin nuts?" I shouted and threw back the midget device.

"Why?" he asked waving his hands.

"You think you can insert this in the USB port of the comp right in the middle of the lab??"

"Yes" he said and smiled.

"How?? All those invigilators are your butler is it??" I asked wishing it was true. Butlers in white standing beside us in the lab serving us a pen-drive each on a silver tray... A plastic smile would've been bearable then.

"Well... Good if that happens... Otherwise also I'll do it... I'll have to..." he said with his eyes fixed on the savior device.

"You know if you're caught you'll get an year's suspension... Two invigilators for just twenty students... Fucking around is impossible..."

"Why don't you think of it this way? Just two invigilators for twenty students... Fucking around is possible..." he said as his brow furrowed, "I'll take my chances Ali... It's a pass or a suspension... No fail option in this..."

A frown on Sandy's face... I knew he'd do it.

"Face a fail or have the insanity to do it..." he said and placed the black monster in my hand.

It was simple... The invigilator turns around - You take the thing out of your sock - Insert it into the comp's ass - Copy the code that you've fished out from the lottery... Done.

It was simple... You get through and you pass a lousy exam. You get caught and your career's ruined.

It was simple... Sandy can do it. I can't.

'Everybody... Type the code and get the output verified. As you know malpractice of any kind will attract severe consequences... Check your pockets, pouches, surroundings, even hands and handkerchiefs for any scribbling...' The baldheaded external announced. He didn't mention underwear in his list... Sandy thought socks could've been a little risky.

I sat in front of the blank computer screen... with an equally blank mind.

'Program no. 14' the placard gleefully showed. It had something to do with 'Decimal up-down counter'. The name sounded funny... that's all I knew about it.

I knew I would taste the bitter fruit of 'failing in your professional course' for the first time. Sandy wouldn't. Because he has the balls...and the pen-drive... Both in his undies.

Two external invigilators walked around the lab aisles. They were a typical breed... Potbellied with their shirt buttons having a testing time, blooming moustaches, dooming bald patches... And they were not serving pen-drives on silver trays.

I saw Sandy's face on the other end of the aisle. He saw me with a grave expression, the invigilator turned towards me, he suddenly flashed a disturbingly wide grin... I didn't smile.

"Sir! The output..." Sandy's voice came from the other end. The screen in front of me had all the random words I could remember from the last bench attendance of the Microprocessors' classes. It took me an hour to fill the screen somehow... the brain was still blank.

'Hmmm... Okay... Output verified... You may go for viva...' I heard one of the examiners tell him.

'Sandy passed. I won't...' I thought looking at the scene. The nerd in me had broken out of the shell... I wished I could pass somehow... There was desperation...*some-fuckin-how.*

I heard Sandy's steps as he walked through the aisle behind my chair.

"Ahem..." he noisily cleared his throat and I felt the cold black-midget-monster slip down my back through the collar of my shirt.

My head suddenly turned towards Sandy... He wide-grinned while walking away. I smiled. He winked.

In a flash of a moment, I had all thirty programs lying in my shirt.

I now needed the guts. I hoped he had dropped that too inside...

With shaky hands, I enclosed the 'pass or suspend' device in my fist. I looked around the lab. Their bald heads were facing me...faces facing the other side.

'Fuck it Ali... Do it!' - I filled the computer's hole... Bang copy... Bang eject... Bang it disappeared into my sock... Done.

I turned around. The potbelly lay inches close to my nose... He stood staring at me.

With a numb mind and numb face, I looked at him.

His fat mole had three thick hairs jutting out... That was all I could make out from the moment. I had dried... in my throat and in my brain.

The face bent down and came where the pot was, "I think you're too tense... There's still an hour left... Relax and try getting the output..." he smiled and left.

Before I could realise, the 'pass or suspend' device had chosen the former for me.

The dryness disappeared... I was through.

"Sir! The output..." My voice echoed through the lab.

"Thank you sir..." I said and left... I had to thank him!

"You're one piece of shit man... What the fuck are you made up of you prick..." I shouted frantically and jumped on Sandy's figure on the bed just as I entered the room after exam.

"Hey Ali... What the fuck! Hey c'mon..." he reacted as if his boxer clad body was gonna be raped.

"You've saved me Sandy... You don't know the good you did to me... You're the most impossibly best buddy I'll ever have *yar*..." I said and collapsed over his bed.

"I know the good I've done... And just a best buddy won't do you ass... This calls for a treat at the best pub..." he said as I lit a fag.

"And get off the bed... I'm not Surender or Virender... Go celebrate with them..." he said laughing.

"Fuck everyone and fuck the world..." I shouted into the smoke. Finally, 'the ghost called MP lab' had died.

Other ghosts hadn't. I realised I had forgotten to switch on the phone that I had switched off inside the cabin with Divya a day before. It went on... And it beeped.

'u r such a dog ali... i waited for ur call or atleast a msg... n u dint even bother to talk back... fuck off n dont show me ur face again...'

I stared into the screen.

"Shit man... I forgot to call Divya..." I said looking at Sandy.

"So call now... Big deal..."

"I'm in trouble *yar*... She was anyways pissed with me... And now she won't even pick the call..."

"Then you're fucked... But why did you two break up?" he asked peeping out of the blanket.

"What!! When did I say break up?? I said she's pissed... and that's because I'm not signing some lousy undertaking..."

"What?? Undertaker?? That wrestler?? You know he..."

"Fuck you! I said undertaking... Forget it... You won't understand..."

"Ya... I don't wanna understand... But what undertaking and all are you involved in??"

"The undertaking is that..." I said and stopped.

"It's some petty stuff *yar*... Nothing much... You go to sleep..." I said and tiredly threw myself into the bed.

I thought of the morning in Dr. Verma's cabin. Her stern face and her walking away figure that never turned back.

Some ghosts had died... Some deadlier ones were still alive. And they weren't petty.

Shit Happens

TO WHOM IT MAY CONCERN:

`I (the signatory), undertake the responsibility, solely and wholly, for any effect of the surgery (details enclosed) on the diseased (details enclosed). I understand that I will not hold National Institute of Mental Sciences answerable, in any regard, even in case of death of the patient, under any circumstances. I understand the gravity of this document and I've read and understood all the details/leaflets attached along with the same. I signature it under no influence of pressure/intimidation/force by any means whatsoever.'`

I signed the dotted line and slid back the stack of sheets to the doctor sitting opposite.

"Thanks Mr. Ali..." he said and got up, "This is Dr. Mathew... Subordinate-head, Neurology."

I shook his hand and looked at his face properly for the first time. He was young and resembled one of the framed images hung in Dr. Verma's cabin. But he seemed less beastly and more humane than the panda creature... Or at least his handshake did.

"I assume you've read through the document in detail..." he asked looking into the papers.

"Yes... I read it..." I mumbled... I hadn't.

"So let me brief you on this once more..." He said and started scribbling into his notepad, "The surgery is scheduled around a month from now at present ... In this we'll use the concept of monitored resonant electrical waves on the subject's brain cells... As stated the procedure is experimental and to minimize the possibility of any fatal outcome on the subject, Dr. Verma is going to supervise it... The subject right now is..."

"Okay I got it..." I said abruptly, unable to tolerate the medical jargon.

"As you wish... It is our obligation to brief the signatory about the details..." he said pushing his notepad back.

"Dr. Thomas... Can I ask you something?" I said getting up to leave.

"Ya sure... And my name's Mathew... Not Thomas..."

"Do you know the name of the subject?"

"What?? The name?? No actually that you can check at the..."

"It's okay" I said and left.

'i signed the undertaking... now dont act pricey and come down... im standing down...' After three unanswered rings, I messaged her standing below the women's hostel building.

Standing there, waiting to see her again, I realized that the clauses in the undertaking failed to concern me. I wanted her. She concerned me... And I was ready to sign any damned dotted line for that to happen.

'im not comin anywhere... never again talk to me ali... listen to me for once... its over between us... forget me... pls dont try contacting...'

The words on the screen blew my head apart like an explosion. I looked around in disbelief. Everything suddenly muted. Pitch darkness hit my eyes and a strong seizure squeezed my head... Literally. It was happening. A pair of hands shutting hard on my eyes. I turned around. She stood smiling.

"Hey preppy…"

"Oh… Why do you wanna kill me Divya?" I gasped looking at her face.

"Hmm… I don't wanna kill you and all… Ya but your pale face looks so funny…" she said and giggled.

My face looked funny I knew. Her's looked beautiful like always… I knew.

A cool morning breeze pushed her hair waywardly all over her face. She smiled and I realized what I was missing for the last two days… a look in her eyes.

"Let's get out of here… No one should see me here with you…" she said tugging back her hair.

"What?? Why?? What did I do??" I asked in surprise.

"Not you… I mean any guy… This is the girl's hostel area you dumbo…" she said and pulled me towards the bike.

I beamed with pride as she sat behind the RX without saying a word. I couldn't remember the last time it happened.

"Don't be too happy… Scooty keys are upstairs… That's why I'm sitting behind your aged bike…" She said and it continued… I still couldn't remember the last time it happened.

"So… How was your prac exam?" She asked as we settled into the Emergency block cafeteria.

The smell wasn't the same as it was on the 'bad result' night. There were people around, there were noises around. The earlier smell of emptiness was today filled by the smell of bustling crowd of visitors.

"Prac was good… Actually quite easy…" I said leaning back on the plastic chair.

"It was good? How? You said you wouldn't even pass..."

"I studied properly the night before... I was so engrossed in studies that I couldn't even remember to message or call you..." I said trying a sober look. The examiner's hairy mole flashed in front of me for a split second...

"Why are you smiling? What is it?" She asked seeing a sudden smirk on my face.

"Hmmm... Okay I'll tell you something..." I said leaning forward.

"What?"

"Hmmm... Do you know what a pen-drive is?" I said and leaned back ready to hear oodles of praises for my guts and her reactions of disbelief.

"Shit! Why didn't you get caught??" She said and thumped the table. The jug spilled some water. I looked at her jaw dropped... She giggled.

"Don't you find it such a gutsy thing to do? I mean look at the risk I took..." I said trying to get at least a fleeting response of dignity for my job.

"Gutsy? Ali... You know what? You've signed the undertaking... That is a gutsy thing to do..." She said with her face suddenly turning serious.

I let her words slowly settle into me. A poking unease ran down as I looked at her blankly.

"What?? You didn't sign it?? Ali?" She asked shaking me out of thought.

"Ya... Ya I signed it... I signed it Divya..." I mumbled.

"So? What happened to you? Imagine Ali... If Gopal becomes alright... You'll be his hero like forever..." She said and smiled.

"Hmmm... I gotta go... I'll come later..." I said and suddenly got up pushing the chair back.

"Whoa! All of a sudden?? What happened to you??" She asked taken aback.

"Nothing... I've some work... I'll go... Bye..." I said and walked away.

"Ali... Wait!" her voice called out from behind as I reached outside.

She walked up to me and held my hand, "I know what's bothering you... Take it easy... Just remember that I love you..." She said looking straight into my eyes.

"Now go... Get lost..." She giggled and left my hand.

"Bye..." I said and sped off.

Riding away from NIMS Campus, I realized it wasn't only hard for me to love Divya, it was getting addictive. I had fallen into more of an addiction than in love with her.

I was ready to hold the responsibility of someone's death just for a look in her eyes. I was signing death documents just for a feel of her hands.

I loved Gopal and never wanted to put myself and him into this. There was a childhood Ali in me who screamed that I had gone self-seeking to an awful level. I pacified him saying that Gopal would be back and never let myself think of the other possibility. If his surgery-bed turned into death-bed...the screams would never stop.

The phone beeped as I braked the bike in front of the hostel.

'ali... something i couldn't say in front of u... i feel terrible that I pushed u into signing... i kno im the reason u did it... but believe me i made u sign coz i kno this is what even u wanted... the risk is jus the part of med science... so relax n dont think much... there's still a month left... u're a good person at heart preppy... luv u... :) (n now dont u dare let it go to ur head)'

I read the message and tried to hold back what she dared me on. I couldn't.

"Hey! When is the treat?" Sandy asked as I entered the room.

"Treat for what?? What are you talking about??" I said and ducked to avoid the slipper.

"Fuckola man… This place rocks… Look at that one… She's fuming hot…" Sandy said pointing for the fifth time at the same girl.

"Sandy! I know she's hot goddamnit… There are others also…"

It wasn't his fault. He was drunk… And she was hot.

The place was Legends of Rock, the pub had the similar dimly lit ambiance, with booze flowing on the tables and in the menu. But with liquor for the livers it also served the classic 60's rock for the senses.

I sat there munching the chicken drumsticks and waited for Sandy to finish the beer pitcher all by himself. Last time he gulped down two before throwing up.

I never found anything hateful about booze and puke parties. I always liked friends around me raising glasses to kick a toast… but somehow I could never fill my glass with the bitter fluid. There was no preachy reason to it. But I just couldn't drink… And I know I never will.

"Hey… Come to the campus… Soon… I'll wait…" Divya said on the phone.

"Hmmm… Not now Divya… I'm outside…" I shouted into the microphone as loud music blared around.

"Outside? Where outside?"

"L.O.R…"

"What??"

"L.O.R. as in Legends of Rock… that pub…" *It was always hip to call it LOR.*

"Okay… Come in an hour if you can… Or I'm leaving for Mumbai for a month… Bye…" She said and hung up.

"What the fuck!" I mumbled looking around.

"Hey listen… Divya…" I called up again.

"Bye… One hour… Come soon…" She disconnected.

I looked down and gasped, it was impossible to reach NIMS in an hour, and with a drunk Sandy sitting on the pillion, reaching with all your limbs in place was a good job done.

"Hey Ali… Check out that babe man…" Sandy said patting my shoulder.

"I don't wanna see… You drink fast and we'll leave…" I said pushing down his hand.

"Fuck… She's looking this way… Just turn around and see once…" He said and thumped down his glass on the table.

"Fuck dude… Those babes are walking towards our table… Just turn around once… Seriously…" he continued looking over my shoulder.

"You shut up and drink…" I said looking at him.

"Ali… Am I hallucinating or those two girls are really standing just behind you right now?" he said looking above.

"Where?" I asked turning back.

"Hey preppy…" She patted my face.

"Close your mouth dumbo…" She said and giggled.

"Hey… Divya… Oh my god… Come sit…" I said sinking in the shock… It was getting habitual.

"Hi Ali..." the other girl said.

"Hi..." Sandy replied before me.

Again, it wasn't his fault. He was drunk... And she was super-hot.

This doesn't happen often when I'm with Divya, but I was distracted, the chinky babe she carried along with her into the pub was a hormone stirrer. Black nailed and pierced brow with a short skirt that ended well on the better side of her knees. Sandy's eyes were glued on her... I managed to look away.

"Hmmm... Ali... This is Tenzin... Remember??" Divya said laughing.

"Oh... Hi Tenzin..." Sandy again pitched in.

"Hi..." she said and bent sideways to tie her stiletto-sandal strap that wrapped half of her leg. Sandy stared into the tumbling neckline... I too.

Divya and I chatted while Sandy's eyes never let off the commitment. Soon half of the menu stood on table with Sandy and Tenzin thumping down vodka glasses one after another.

"I wasn't kidding... I'm going to Mumbai..." Divya said leaning over my shoulder as I helplessly saw 250 bucks tequila shots appearing and disappearing as fast.

"When?? Now??" I asked trying to get something out of all the money Tenzin was gulping down... Seeing her cleavage was becoming boring now.

"No dumbo... Otherwise how could I come to meet you now? I've got to go next week..."

"Next week when?? For how many days??" I asked as my phone beeped.

It was Sandy - 'fuck ali... this females super sexy man... just bend down for some reason n check out her thighs... hooh...'

I looked at him. "Oh! Matchbox fell down…" he said and stooped under the table.

"Did you hear?? I'm saying I'm going on 24th Jan…" Divya suddenly interrupted as I tried to push my phone off the table edge.

"Ya… Ya… I heard… And when you coming?" I asked fixing my eyes back on her face.

'Ali! Sandy is drunk… You aren't. Look at Divya.' I told myself.

"Ali!! 24th Jan… I'm going on 24th Jan…" She said with her eyes opening up to a double. They were beautiful. She was beautiful. Tenzin is a pig.

"Okay… I know 24th Jan… When are you coming back?" I said again fiddling with the mobile… One look was no harm. Even committed people see FTV.

"Coming back?? You're such an ass… 24th Jan goddamnit…" She said and straightened up.

"24th Jan… So what's special?? Republic day is on 26th right??"

"You forgot my birthday??" She asked and the smile on her face disappeared.

"Hah! I was just messing with you… Obviously I remember your birthday's on 24th Jan…" I said and smiled. She still didn't. Something was wrong. I knew the look… It appears just before I get a punch.

"I said I'm going on 24th Jan… You remember my birthday?? It's on 25th Jan you ass…" she said and her fist came charging towards me. I let her hit. She hits softly now… Or I love her more now.

"Okay sorry… I admit it slipped off my mind… But birthdays and all don't matter… You know I love you… Now smile and cheer up…" I said and pulled her towards me.

Sandy smiled. His matchbox again fell. We both bend down to pick it up.

"So Ali… Thanks for the partyyyyy…" Tenzin said while getting up to leave with Divya.

"It was Sandy's party… Thank him…" I said pointing at his drowsy face. Boozard girls are always easy to lay, chinki is an added advantage. Perfect kind of true love for Sandy.

"Oh… Thanks Sandy…" She lunged forward and shook his hand. The stiletto-booze combo was misbalancing her and she almost tripped onto my lap. Divya held her back and smiled at me… I whined.

"But what is the treat for Sandy?" She asked getting back.

"The treat?? The treat was for… wait… FUCK THE EDUCATION!!" Sandy's drunk voice suddenly erupted into the pub. Tenzin got half her senses back.

I tried to pull down his hand while people looked at his beer mug raised into the air. Nobody responded… Just Divya's laughter echoed.

"Okay guys... FUCK THE WORLD!!" He tried again and all the glasses around flew up in the air.

"Fuck the world!!" hoarse sounds and glass-clashes repeated after him and surpassed the heavy music.

My wallet had suffered a near-death experience with vodka glasses visiting the table like teacups… But the treat suddenly became Sandy's.

"Okay we've to go… It's late… Bye Ali… Bye Sandy…" Divya said pulling Tenzin away from the table while I looked at her face.

She walked back and bowed down to my ear, "I know you were staring… You are such a dog preppy…" She whispered giggling.

"Bye…" She said and walked away. I blankly looked at her crooked smile until the most addictive drink in the pub disappeared out of the doorway.

I turned back… "Fuck the world!" Some fools were still responding.

"Come we'll go… I don't wanna pay 100 bucks cleaning charges…"

I told Sandy pulling him from the couch. Getting too close to him could've been messy now. He doesn't signal before throwing up... Last time it was Happy's face.

"Ya... Coming..." He got up and clung on to my shoulder.

"Bye guys..." He waved to the pub crowd with his hand going wayward.

"Fuck the world!" Some were still hung on to it... Booze makes you slow-witted.

"Sit straight... If you trip off in middle of the road then don't expect me to pick you up okay..." I shouted back to Sandy whose body had turned into a sack of potatoes... Free booze and high liver capacity don't go well together either.

We reached the hostel and I dropped Sandy on his bed. I took out the Navy-Cut pack from his pocket and lit a fag. After almost a week the cigarette smoke felt good. I could call myself a non-smoker now... Except these exceptions. Which happened a little too often.

"You know Ali... You love her..." Sandy said lying aimlessly on his bed. Staring at the equally aimless mosquitoes.

"What?? You're awake?? I thought you had passed out..." I asked turning to him.

"I'm alive now... The booze was amazing..." He said with a dozy voice and sat up on his bed.

"And so was Tenzin..." he said and coughed out a laugh.

"Tenzin?? Ya... She's hot..." I murmured looking at his face. It seemed different. I had either seen a grin or a frown there. This expression was new to his face. He looked sad...and funny.

"You alright?" I asked him from a safe distance. Maybe he was just about to throw up.

"Fuck you... I'm okay... I won't puke..." He said and lit a new cigarette for himself. Three years and this never happened...two different cigarettes when we were together. The only thing that bonded us as friends was the fighting for the last puff of the stick. I loved the times. I loved Sandy... Especially after the lab case, I would be a jackass if I didn't.

"What happened to you?" I went and patted his cheek.

"Nothing *yar*..." He said and took out a small picture frame from his drawer.

I never knew Sandy had shoulder length hair. I never knew he once wore black leather pants and buckled jackets. And until some hot chick allows you to dive into her neck and get clicked with her sitting on the bonnet of a Land Cruiser, even the girlfriend and car was his.

"That's you??" I asked looking into the picture... Curvy ass.

"No that's my dad... And that's mom... Nice *na*?" he said and forced a laugh.

I too tried to laugh... Long legs.

"The bitch dumped me..." He said with his bloodshot eyes suddenly fixing on me.

Before I could react... They turned into brimmed swimming pools. Sandy was crying. Again a first in three years.

"Sandy... Hey..." I stuttered trying to find correct words as streams rolled out of his eyes. Sandy was uglier than I thought.

"Shit! These are not tears... This is some reaction of those tequila shots..." He said and wiped off his eyes.

I laughed and dropped the photo frame back into his drawer. He too laughed. The grin on his face returned.

"But at least tell me something about the pic..." I asked. I knew it would pain him...but knowing about the girl would've been interesting.

"I know you wanna know about her you jackass..." he said and patted my back. I stumbled. His pats were becoming heavier every day.

"Those were my twelfth standard days... My money use to define me... Whatever friends I got were actually my money's friends... And same was the case with girlfriends... She too loved my money and I knew that... But the mistake I did was I started loving her..." He said and stopped.

"Forget it... Shit happens..." he said getting up.

"So... You liked Tenzin??" I asked trying to get him off his nostalgia. Seeing Sandy cry somehow upset me. Though his wide grin was the most irritating thing ever invented by man... It looked better on his face than tears.

"Tenzin?? Tenzin is great body great ass... Nice petite chink... And amazing legs..." he dropped the matchbox off the table and winked at me. I laughed. He roared.

"But you know what? Tenzin and Divya are different... Tenzin is like porn... Divya is like love..." He said looking at me, "And you love her... She loves you... You're lucky enough..."

"But love's all bullshit... As Eminem says..." He said and plugged the woofers into his Pod.

'But I do know one thing though
Bitches, they come they go
Saturday through Sunday, Monday
Monday through Sunday yo
Maybe I'll love you one day
Maybe we'll someday grow
'Til then just sit your drunk ass
on that fuckin runway ho'

I looked at him as he tried to do his random clumsy movements that he loved to call dance. I knew he never wanted me to discuss that photo frame again. The booze in his bowel had spoken up…not him.

He was trying to forget what he deliberately kept in his drawer and saw day in day out. The long locks, the leather apparel, the Land Cruiser…everything was gone. It's funny what love does to people… Even to people like him.

"Come… Dance… Imagine I'm Tenzin… Whooo…" He shouted towards me revolving in his boxers. Tenzin would have looked better.

I wanted her to stay

"So what gift are you gonna buy me??" Divya's loud voice attracted a few glances... Or maybe her elegant satin shirt did.

It was 11 pm into the night... But airports never sleep. Divya was leaving to Mumbai for a month... I was sad.

"Gift?? I could've bought you but you won't be here tomorrow... So all I can say is the same old cliché... Happy birthday in advance..." I said smirking at her.

"You could've bought me?? You'll have to buy me a very expensive gift..." She said pushing me away. Gentle pushs... I loved them.

Her face glowed under the bright focus lamps. While the black satin shirt and clung on jeans would've made her top any goddamn airhostess test right there, my as usual rugged looks wouldn't have even passed me for a steward... They became further rugged with her standing next to me. I loved that.

"Okay... What do you want? I've...hmmm...50 bucks right now." I said taking out my wallet. I wished two ice-creams from the nearby stall could've ended the gift discussion.

"Okay... 50 would be enough... Let me get two ice-creams..." She said and took the note from my hand.

I tried to stay calm and not jump frantically in the air under the disbelief of the moment. Fifty rupee note was my lowest ever. Even a Navy-Cuts pack for Sandy costed me more.

"Here's your ice-cream..." She said handling me half of the gift... Even better.

"So... What would you gift me when I come back??" she asked swigging in on the cone.

I looked at her face as I suddenly landed hard on the ground.

"Divya... I thought this itself was... I mean..."

"Shit! Are you nuts? These ice-creams are your gift?? Ali!!" she said with her eyes again opening up to a double... I don't want her to go.

"See Divya... Diamonds can never give you the delight of these small joys in life okay... Money and all shouldn't matter when it's true lo..." A punch stopped my blabbering.

"Ali... I'll have to check-in now... You better leave..." She said as we stood in front of the domestic terminal. The time had come. She looked at me. I looked at her. Her eyes pooled. *I wanted her to stay.*

"Hmmm..."

"You're okay no..." She said and held my hands.

"Ya I'm fine..." I mumbled.

"Ali... Keep this in your pocket... Read it after I go..." She said passing me a folded paper. I looked at her face... *I wanted her to stay.*

"One month would be too long..." I said dropping down my head.

There was a silence. I didn't move. She came forward and hugged me. And then, standing in middle of the busy airport porch...we kissed.

I pulled her close to me as heads turned towards us. The hurriedly rushing busy people were no more busy. Again, the bright lights, the noisy airport, the fixed eyes...everything ceased to matter. She mattered.

"Love you preppy..." She said settling back her hair. She was in tears. I wanted her to smile. *I wanted her to stay.*

"Bye..." I said and turned back.

Curbing the urge to look back as I walked away from the porch… I realized how difficult being in love can get.

~

'Ali… The surgery will be within two weeks… And as I won't be there for a month… You'll have to visit alone… Listen to me… You just need to relax… Everything will be okay. I couldn't postpone my visit… Parents just don't listen to any excuse. So just take it easy on yourself… I'll be there very soon…

And I never wanted to say this… And please don't mention it in any call or message either… But it'd be better if we face the worst case possible now itself…

If he dies… Just forget it.

Don't take it too hard on yourself… Just keep it out of your head until I come there…

Love you,

Divya'

I read her letter and tossed the paper aside.

Lying on the bed, worn-out and sleepless, I realised I was too tired to even react to the thunderous words in the letter.

She had put it straight and clear… I couldn't.

Maybe that's what they teach in medical colleges.

'If he dies… Just forget it'

I wished he was a 'subject' to me too.

Under sheer sleeplessness and exhaustion, I forcibly shut my eyes and tried to visualize her smiling face.

Sleep.

"Hey preppy... Wish me wish me..." Her shrill voice cut through the microphone... And my sleep.

"Okay I wish you... Now let me sleep... I'll call you when I get up..." I said turning aside.

"What okay I wish you? Say happy birthday... Say say..." Her hyper-energy was pouring out of the microphone. What is it about birthdays that continue to excite people year after year?

"Happy birthday Divya..." I said smiling within. I wished I could go to NIMS and meet her.

"Okay get up and do as I say..." she said with an authoritative tone that I had grown habitual to.

"Ya... I'll do as you say... But when I get up... So for now shall I go back to sleep??"

"Ali!! Do as I say... Get up! Now!" A little too loud. A little too authoritative... My eyes opened up in a flash.

"Do what?? Its 6 am Divya??" I asked looking at the alarm clock.

"Get up from your bed first! Get up Ali... Listen to me..."

"What is it? First tell me..." I asked finally sitting up. Apart from nature's call, it was only her call that could get me out of the bed at 6 am.

"Get up and dress up... Don't say a word... Buy a gift for me and deliver it to Tenzin in NIMS..." She said and giggled. I didn't. This wasn't funny. Atleast to me.

"Divya... It's 6 am... I came back late last night... You'd have just reached home now and started all this?? I'll..."

"I didn't ask you the time preppy... You're gonna do it or not??" She cut me short.

"No" I said… trying to sound stern.

"Ali… Do you love me? I'll call up Tenzin in half-an-hour and ask if you came… Bye…"

"But listen…" Cut.

I knew this was some 'what can you do for me' test that supposedly establishes the degree of your love. She once told me that a guy ran five kilometers to NIMS Campus just to prove his love to her friend. I said he proved his dumbness. Poor fellow could've just hitch-hiked or used a bike. But it's true… Loves makes the world go round. And sometimes people.

Feeling just like that guy, I tried to ignite the cold RX engine in the foggy morning.

"Where do I buy the gift from?? Its 6am…" I called her with battering teeth.

"Oh… So you're going? Good… And since no shop would be open now, I'll be kind to you… Just go and deliver anything… Anything you can find at this time…"

"Anything what??"

"Anything like…hmmm… the newspaper…"

"What???"

"Yes… Become a newspaper boy for a day… Go handover today's newspaper to Tenzin… I just want you to go…"

"Divya actually this is not funny you know… Don't you think you're stretching it a bit too far??"

She disconnected.

Now feeling worse than that guy, I zipped through the fog with the chill numbing my face and fists.

'Sorry Manju-bhai…' I muttered to the closed shutter of Sutta-point and flicked the rolled newspaper lying in front of it.

Here I was, I thought as I rode through the road, ready to steal newspapers and deliver it to some chinki hippie in the freezing morning cold, all for her one phone call.

"Where is Tenzin? I'm standing at the main road… Tell her to come fast…" I shouted on the phone as I looked around.

"Don't shout preppy… Tenzin says she's too lazy to go down… You go and give it to her in the hostel… Room number 12B… Number 12 on the first floor…"

It took me some time to believe what I heard.

"What!!" I reconfirmed.

"Room number 12B… Go and give it to her…"

"What!!"

"Ali… Go to the girl's hostel… Nobody will catch you… Everybody's gone home… Only that room is open… Go now…"

"Enough Divya… What the hell is your…"

She had disconnected.

I looked around in disgust and gasped into the fog.

'you love me no?' her message beeped on the phone.

It took this one question from someone, dug deep in her bed and blanket some thousand miles away, to get me out of the bed fighting the morning cold and follow a series her silly orders like a dummy.

After several unanswered rings and randomly shouting 'Tenzin Tenzin' at the hostel building, hoping her head would pop out of one of the windows, I surrendered to the reality. The trap laid out by Divya was not to fail…

Girls' hostel was the only place I had not visited on NIMS Campus… Not anymore.

I walked into the entrance, there was a security guard's chair... Sadly no security guard.

I hurriedly scaled the flight of stairs that led to the first floor, tightly clutching the deadly combat weapon I had - a rolled newspaper.

The galleries were empty and quiet, I slowly walked towards the increasing room numbers. 10B... 11B... 12B... Divya was right. 12B was the only room that wasn't bolted with a lock...though I wished it was.

I touched the door and it swung open. The room was empty. Two conjoined beds lay in the middle. I stepped inside and looked around with my heartbeat touching a hundred. There was still nobody.

"Tenzin... Are you there? This is Ali here... Are you around??" I hesitantly spoke to the silence.

"Hi Ali..."

I suddenly turned around.

Before I could react, the newspaper dropped... My lips were into hers.

"My flight got cancelled..." She said and my lips again disappeared.

I tried to settle to the shock but everything faded under the wildness of the moment.

We were kissing each other like never before. She hung herself around me and I got pushed to the wall.

I had to breathe... I wanted to see her face again... I wanted to talk to her again...

"Divya... I so love you..." I said gasping for air. Her eyes were inches away from mine with open strands of hair wildly scattered all over her face.

I stood stuck against the wall with her legs wrapped around my waist. I was carrying her in my arms... the world would've stopped rotating and I wouldn't have given a damn.

"Come out of the shock preppy... This is for real..." She said and thud her forehead against mine.

I loved every word she was saying, every breath she was taking, every twinkle her eyes reflected... I loved her all over again. There was a silence but our eyes continued talking. Our lips continued kissing...

I walked across the room and rested her down on the bed. She kept looking at me with her smile adorned face. I settled back her hair and kissed her forehead... Kissed her.

She pulled me all over her and snuggled upto me.

And somewhere in that passionate kissing and feeling the warmth of each other's bodies... We were out of our clothes.

She was out of her satins and I was out of my ruggedness... I went down on her.

We made love.

"Ali… Get up!" Her voice shook me from sleep.

I looked around... For a change I woke up in a girl's hostel room. For a change my eyes opened up to her face in front of me… I looked inside the blanket, for a change I was stark naked.

"Divya!" I almost shouted.

"What??" She said tying her hair. She was dressed with her luggage bags ready. I was lying nude in Tenzin's blanket.

"Why didn't you wake me?" I said wrapping around the only cover I had.

"You looked kinda cute while sleeping preppy…" She said looking into the mirror hanging on the wall.

With sweat beads sprouting on my face, I slid out of the bed and dropped to the floor, somehow reached out for my underpants and pants, slipped into them and let out a sigh of relief… It's not easy being nude, especially when the person in front of you is all dressed… She looked gorgeous.

"Where are you going?" I asked standing up straight with pride. I was pants-on now.

"My flight is at 11 am… We'll have to rush… I called a cab…" She said walking towards me and kissed my cheek… She smelled great.

"What?? It's 9 already…" I said looking into the watch. Only three hours had passed. Acting the newspaper boy in the morning seemed like a distant memory now… Thankfully.

After almost a hundred checks and re-checks in the mirror and 'am I looking fine?' questions, she moved out of the room. I pulled the trolley.

"What if there's any security guard downstairs?" I asked looking at her glossed face… She was too beautiful to wear make-up.

"I hope there is…" She said smirking at me, "I'll simply tell him I don't know you..."

I kept looking at her... I had forgotten what I asked.

"Okay don't worry... I'll fight him..." She said and ruffled my hair.

We moved out of the hostel entrance with the same chair again guarding the premises... I felt like leaving a 'thank you' note for the guard.

"Oh! The cab came..." She said looking at the white Indica parked outside the hostel compound.

The driver came and took the trolley from my hand. The same situation struck again... *I wanted her to stay.*

"9.30... I can't wait a minute more... I'll have to go Ali..." She said holding my hands.

"Go..." I smiled at her and kissed her cheek.

"And oh I almost forgot... Here's one more note for you..." She said and passed a folded paper into my hand.

"Love you..." She said and turned around to walk.

Feeling like a lifeless body, I stood in middle of the compound until the cab disappeared into the greens.

'My flight didn't get cancelled preppy... I cancelled the ticket and rescheduled it to the later flight... All this just to see you again...

And I told you to deliver a newspaper as my birthday gift... Forcing you out of your bed early morning and you were so annoyed...

So who loves whom more??

Love you always,

Divya'

I soothed the creases of the paper and slipped it into my pocket.

The long walk from the hostel compound to the bike parking seemed beautiful.

The early morning breeze, the tall trees swaying to the wind, the never ending straight road… Everything seemed anew.

I reread the note and ran my fingers on the words written by her.

Life seemed anew... She was beautiful. And she was mine.

If he dies... Just forget it.

"Ali... Wake up!" Sandy was shaking me in a dream.

"Ali... Wake up you ass!!" He continued shaking me.

"Ali... Listen!" He slapped me... My eyes opened in a flash. It wasn't a dream.

"What the fuck! Did you just slap me?" I asked rubbing my cheek.

"You were not getting up... I thought you died..." He said passing my cellphone into my hand.

"Divya has been calling you since early morning... After some hundred rings I picked up... She told me to wake you up anyhow and tell you to call her back immediately..." He said and went back to bed.

With sticky eyes, I looked around the room, stretched out my body and called her.

"Ali... Where are you?" She asked before I could speak a word.

"Hostel... Why?" I mumbled rubbing my eyes.

"Are you mad? What are you doing there?"

"Hmmm... Sleeping before talking to you..."

"Sleeping?? Go to NIMS Ali... Rush..."

"Why? You came back from Mumbai?"

"No... Don't you know what happened??"

"What happened??"

"Ali... Gopal... The surgery happened today morning... It was successful Ali... He's okay... Go to NIMS..."

I was silent. I sat listening to whatever she was saying like a stone. The more she spoke into the microphone, the more my mind fell into a trance.

"...Imagine Ali... Your friend is cured... Go meet him... Are you there? Say something... Ali..."

She kept talking.

I cut the call. Picked the RX keys. Ran out of the room... Faster than ever.

The bike slowed down in front of the neurology building... My pulse didn't.

Long galleries, echoing sounds, brisking white figures... nothing seemed to register.

I scaled the lengthy staircases and ran to the ICU section panting for breath...

The blurry vision of a white coat resolved into Dr. Verma's body. I stood gasping in front of him clutching my knees...

My mind was occupied. My breath was away. I didn't know what to say... How to say, "Hi..." I said looking at his grumpy face.

"Who are you?" His throaty voice echoed around me.

I stood up straight looking at his face. I stared hard. He was the same panda creature. I'm bad at remembering faces but his beasty looks were a spot on match.

"Dr. Verma... I'm Ali... I met you once... About the undertaking of..."

"Oh Ali... You are the friend right? You are coming now?" He said with his heavy hand on my shoulder.

"Ya now... I wasn't informed... Nobody called me... How is Gopal? I mean the patient... I wanna meet him..." I said feeling a strong urge to twist his hand and push him down the high gallery. I hated him.

"What?? You wanna meet him?? You can't meet him… He's dead…" He said and his hand didn't move. His smile didn't fade. Neither did the sharp texture of his wrinkles.

I looked at him… My mind faded. I moved.

The next thing I knew was Dr. Verma's face pulled up inches away from mine with my hands gripping hard on his coat-collar. Some filthiest of expletives roared out of my mouth. Three men strongly held my hands and back and were trying to pull me away… I wanted to kill him.

I was pulled back.

I shouted frantically. The panda just stared… I screamed frantically. But he just stared.

My mind had gone numb. My body had gone wild.

Gopal can't die.

Minutes passed… Gopal hadn't died.

"Listen Ali... You took Dr. Verma's words literally... The surgery was successful and your friend's fine..." I looked at Dr. Mathew's speaking mouth.

A glass of cold water into my throat and on my face had rested me. Somebody had jabbed a sharp-punch hard into my back to make me let off the panda's collar... The pain was biting the spot. I was tired.

"He said he's dead... That's why I jumped over him..." I said noticing my words were getting irregular and unstrung. I wanted to run out in the open.

Dr. Mathew's face was humble and humane... It was the only thing that kept me fixed on the couch in his stuffy cabin.

"Ali listen..." he came and sat next to me, "Your friend isn't dead... But in a way he is... Not as a person but as your friend... Let me explain to you in simple words... Our procedure was extensive but experimental... We tried to stimulate the dead neurons in the subject's brain by electrically resonant waves... It worked... Everything went well... His brain will function well within a few weeks... But it is refreshed... He can't recall anything from the past... Not even his name... In medical circles we mockingly call this phenomenon as 'successful surgery but dead patient'... So Dr. Verma telling you that he's dead means he's dead for you... And for anybody who knew him... We're barring anyone from visiting him now because that can strain him as his mental state is extremely sensitive at present."

He looked at me. My mind registered every word he spoke. It was hard for me to react. His eyes waited for my first reaction after his long jargoned speech... I could've cried. But tears again failed to come up. My dry eyes looked at him and I waited for my mind to react...

With an expressionless face... I got up and walked off.

Hungry for fresh air, I strode through the galleries and stairs and finally the roof over my head ended... The thoughts didn't.

I leisurely walked on the long road aimlessly staring at the distant horizon, and tried to understand the moment... The vision blurred. I noticed a pepperiness in my eyes... And at last tears rolled out.

The blurred vision gave way for a series of images and voices... I missed the train with Raghu. I went to a nursing home next day and *we met.* I visited NIMS for the first time. I crouched to the dusty window and saw a face.

The dots of my actions were connecting. Every incident... Eye to eye.

Tears rolled out. The taste was sweet and sour... Just like the memories.

I owed five thousand bucks to Abdullah. I still owe. She came into my life. Beautiful things happened. My dark and gloomy life got filled by her laughter and smiles. She was the most beautiful thing that ever happened to me.

And she will always be...

I bit my lip to confirm this was all a reality... It was... Coz reality bites.......*Sometimes with jagged teeth.*

The taste was sweet and sour... Just like the memories.

Epilogue

"Shut up and sit preppy... Don't ask questions..." Divya shouted as the scooty sped through a deserted Bangalore road.

One month isn't a long time. And again, some things had changed... And some hadn't... Like they never do.

My story had ended up pretty well, I thought... Here I was, revisited my past in a crazy turmoil of events, and now hungry for some fresh whiff of future... For it looked good, atleast from a distance.

Raghu had been the same. While I, like most others, kept on wondering what transformed him that way, he caught everyone unawares when he announced he had cracked the prestigious IAS exam on his Graduation Day. I and Sandy, again like most others, just clapped sitting in the audience. In his parting note, the most silent and deep guy I've ever met, said only one thing – "I'll miss Bangalore. Not because of this college, not because of the days, not because of the friends, but just for one reason... For one face... And for the plight of one life." I knew what he was talking about. A prostitute had changed his life... And for good I guess.

"Take care Ali. I'll get back in touch. And you too Sandy... Hooh, I gotta rush out of this place now." He had said hugging us the tightest ever he could. And the hug, for once, wasn't fake.

Sandy too didn't change much, infact at all. Last time I saw him, his stark naked boxer clad body oscillated up and down on the room's floor, amid some earsplitting music. His phone beeped, I laughed seeing the message – "wat u doin baby? movie tonite? ;)" It was Tenzin. Told you no… Perfect kind of true love for Sandy.

And then, sitting behind the straight moving scooty, jobless as always, my string of thoughts continued.

It's always hard to figure out life, its one thing that fucks itself up, and eventually makes up for that too… All by itself.

Ali too hadn't changed much. Somewhere in the room no. 206, somewhere in the half-tea and Navy-Cut at the Manju-bhai's bench, somewhere in the creaking RX sound, and somewhere in the endless walks at NIMS Campus… Ali will reside forever.

But sometimes, only sometimes, that moment still strikes him, like a hammer with a throbbing force.

For a second, one quote by the great Bob Dylan seemed befitting on life – *'Every pleasures got an edge of pain, so pay for your ticket and don't complain.'*

"Hey… Cool it. Ride slow Divya!" I shouted as a sudden bump jumped me off the seat and off my thoughts.

"Shut up and sit preppy!" She replied.

I laughed to myself, and the ride continued… So did time.

And here finally, I too go off, with one parting note until the next time we meet - *don't complain.*